ONLY ONE WAY

Jannicke Howard

Also by Jannicke Howard:

The Simple Things

ISBN: 978-0-9559923-5-3

PART ONE
The Lull

It was on the day they introduced restricted inter-county travel that Ed's brother Richard had come to visit. Not that it would have hindered either particularly as they both lived in North Yorkshire.

Naomi couldn't say which event stuck in her memory more. Retrospection always played tricks; and no one thought that the restricted travel would come to anything much: it was just a precaution taken by a nanny-state knee-jerking to a hysteric media machine winding the nation up. She always noticed when Richard came to visit though. The beat-up, open-back Landrover appeared on the driveway – certainly kept for functionality more than appearances' sake. It looked like a rust bucket compared to the sleek, glossy four-wheel tanks that the urban rich drove.

From the bedroom window in her first floor flat, Naomi Ellerbeck had a prime position view across the cul-de-sac road to Ed's semi-detached house. Not that she paid particular attention to Ed Stilton most of the time, but she seemed to be in tune with Richard's arrivals. On a day when she was sitting wistfully at the window wishing for something to happen. Then Richard would appear outside and she couldn't help but smile.

She watched Ed come out of the house to greet his brother. Her phone started ringing. Naomi turned away from the window and went to answer the call.

"Naomi?"

She rolled her eyes upon hearing Rudi's voice. There was a time when she hadn't minded hearing from her old flatmate. But recently the situation had changed. He'd grown very strange the last couple of weeks. Paranoid. He rang nearly every day, making absurd demands of her, insisting on evidence that the tasks had been completed when he realised she wasn't taking him seriously.

"Rudi, what a surprise," she joked. "I hope you were happy with the pictures. And I hope this is an end to it. It's the weekend; it's summer and I am very tired of playing games."

"I wish you'd take this seriously;" came the response. "I've told you before; if this comes to nothing, you'll just be storing a lot of tins for me."

"And if it does come to something?"

"Then this will save your life. Or at least give you a fighting chance."

She sighed and glanced across at the bright window. Her flat was so dark and pokey – the sunshine outside was a glaring contrast.

The most worrying part of all of this was not so much what he was asking her to do, but the fact that he was asking at all. Rudi never panicked. Throughout everything the last decade – terrorist attacks, petrol shortages, looming threats of flu pandemics, snow blizzards and all the other minor disasters in between, Rudi never gave the issues a second thought. He carried on as normal. He continued to take all public forms of transport as soon as they were reopened – and to many this was a noticeable act as he lived and worked in London; he never stockpiled food or water, panic-bought petrol, got stressed over the first sneeze, never took antibiotics on principle and was so calm and unbothered by everything that Naomi was sure he put muggers off. He radiated a self-aware certainty that the end was not nigh; that great was his confidence.

He should have been a paramedic or a doctor in A&E of guardian angel proportions. He went to medical school and was ideal for disasters. Instead he'd gone into research and worked at an institute for tropical, rare and highly contagious diseases. The British Centre for Tropical Disease was the official title: tropical being anything obscure or not a regular feature at British G.P. surgery as Naomi understood it. Even that was becoming a less suitable description to bandy around, because people travelled so much. For every health risk that hit the public light, Rudi knew about at least fifty others that the authorities didn't want the media to start flashing around for fear of public panic. Mass hysteria was one of the most feared contagions to people like Rudi.

And still he was cool, unworried, and accepting that things would just work out.

Until about two weeks ago when he'd started this vigil of calls and told her that she needed to start stockpiling. Naomi had presumed it was some kind of nervous breakdown and humoured him on the phone whilst ignoring his advice. He plagued her until she admitted she'd done nothing. She tried to tell him she couldn't afford to buy food on mass, but he would have none of it. He sent her money, told her to go and buy the foods on emailed lists on his behalf. If it turned out she didn't need the food, he would pick it up off her one day. He made her email him photos of the stores in her flat, with her in the picture and dates clearly visible. This was the definition of paranoia.

Her flat wasn't very big, and every patch of available space was now stacked up with supplies. Rows and rows of canned fruit and vegetables, soups and fish with the long use by dates. Dried herbs, dried fruits, pastas, noodles, seaweed. A tray of honey jars – Rudi had been very clear that she needed honey. The small freezer full of meats and fishes – for as long as it would last (Rudi's words). Tea and coffee, bleaches and disinfectants. Surgical spirits, bottles of vodka, brandy and whisky, boxes and boxes of the usual line up of pain killers and medicines (bought from a number of chemists on a number of days – York probably thought she was planning a dramatic suicide attempt at the weekend). Flours and dried yeasts, oils, packets and packets of sugar and salt, vitamin supplements, and a selection of large buckets – she didn't know what he thought she was going to do with those. Neither those nor the bag full of batteries. Stacks of books, torches, bulbs, hammers, nails and screws. She had spent a small fortune.

"How about you, Rudi? Have you got your own stockpile or are you relying on mine?"

"I'm building my own at the flat, but I don't get home that much."

Naomi laughed. "Still married to the job."

"We're pretty secure and well stocked at work. We're all working round the clock at the moment."

"Oh, Rudi. Are you having some kind of breakdown? You make it sound like it's the end of the world. I still can't believe you've bullied me into buying this much crap."

"Well, we'll see."

"Have you heard about the travel restrictions?"

Rudi snorted into the phone. "Stupid idea. It won't help."

"I don't see why they're in place. Is it not just a few sick people down in London? Someone told me it was like the flu."

"There's been a couple of cases in Newcastle."

"What?"

"Amongst other places. But that's not official. Stopping people travelling outside their county is a waste of time. In fact it's a hindrance. It'll only make people panic."

"Exactly, you tell 'em."

"What we need is total lockdown."

"What??!" she laughed. "When was the last time you got some sleep?"

There was silence on the phone for a moment or two. "I don't remember."

"Go to bed."

He ignored her request. "I've got to get back to work. Take care of yourself. I'll be in touch soon."

There was a man at one end of the car park with a longbow. Scrawny, insect-like legs sticking out from the untucked white shirt. An earth coloured waistcoat. Leather hand guard on, making him look like a wannabe boxer with serious misconceptions if one didn't know better. Dark, shaggy hair and thick eyebrows; he had an intense, almost hurt stare.

Naomi pulled up into a space and switched off the engine. Opening the door, she stepped out of her car. "Morning, Ross," she called over to the man with the longbow.

The man seemed to snap out of the day dream on hearing his name.

"You not shooting today?"

Ross wandered over to Naomi's car. She had pushed forward the driver's seat and was angling round the long archery case to pull it out of the vehicle.

"Those wankers are discussing committee decisions and club rules," he said. "We come here to shoot; not bitch. I had to get away from it for a moment."

Naomi smiled wryly as she set her archery case on the ground. "Just ignore them. That's what I do."

"Easier said than done. It drives me up the wall. Such a waste of human life."

Two gangly nineteen year olds carrying compound bow cases – a lot shorter than the traditional English longbow Ross was stood with like a sentry – wandered past, grinning like idiots. "Lucky we shoot outside the city walls, eh, Ross?" they said in passing.

Ross faked a smile at them. "Little wankers. It's the same shit with them every week."

"They only do it because they know it winds you up," Naomi said. She locked her car and picked up her case. "Besides, you only need to worry about me – I'm the only one with a longbow." There was an old York bye-law from days gone by, that it was perfectly within the law to shoot a

Scotsman with your longbow, as long as you were within the city walls. Because Ross was Scottish and a fanatical longbow archer living in York, he took a lot of jokes about this. The joke had worn thin years ago.

"Anyway, I thought you weren't going to be here today," Naomi continued as they wandered across to the outdoor shooting range. "Were you not heading up to Ayr for some family do?"

"Not allowed to. Don't you listen to the news?"

"Oh, of course, restricted inter-county travel." Naomi nodded.

"I wasn't really worried about all this until they brought that in."

"You're worried now?" Naomi sounded disappointed.

"Well, not really," he admitted. "Sarah was getting herself in a flap."

He let the comment hang there. Sarah was the wife, and it was a marriage that wasn't doing too well – at least this was what Naomi presumed from the comments Ross occasionally made; the things he didn't say and the fact that Sarah hadn't shown her face at the archery club for heading on six months. This was where the pair had met, so it had been a common interest. Sarah had started behaving a little strangely about a year ago, skipping meets and eventually quitting altogether. No explanation. Ross wouldn't talk about it.

"What about your mate, Rudi?" Ross changed the direction of conversation. "He works in the health industry. Is he worried?"

Naomi grimaced. "Rudi's having a nervous breakdown. I wouldn't listen to anything he says." Not that Ross and Rudi were going to have a conversation.

"First time they've done this for disease though."

"Done what?"

"Restricted travel."

"Not really."

"What?" Ross laughed. "I missed that one."

"They often restrict travel when there's a foot and mouth case."

"That's animals, Naomi," Ross said. "I was talking about people."

"We're animals too."

They reached the end of the line of archers showing up for a sunny Saturday morning of shooting. A general archery club, with people of all levels and bows turning up. It was mostly a collection of compounds and recurves – shorter and less intimidating bows, with the added advantage of sights. There was a Japanese man who sometimes turned up with a traditional Japanese bow. A couple of committee members also had longbows, but they didn't often shoot with them.

Naomi quickly tied her hair back and put on her wrist guard. She unzipped the case and pulled out her longbow. Setting it up vertical – now taller than she was – she put her foot on one end and started to bend the shaft to string the weapon.

Ross went to get some arrows from his own case that was lying in the grass. "You going to Barrio's this evening?"

Naomi grimaced as she managed to get the bow string in place. She released her foot. "Most probably."

"Might go," Ross muttered.

Naomi smiled to herself. "I thought you weren't into dancing, Ross," she commented as she took her arrows from the case. "Or are you and Sarah taking up a new hobby."

"Sarah won't be going."

Naomi winced and turned away. She should have known better than to mention Sarah. The absent minded comment had just slipped out. She gazed down the length of archers lining up for weekend practice. Malcolm was walking towards them; that stupid green baseball cap on his head as if he thought he was Robin Hood.

"Naomi, Ross," he greeted them. He hadn't brought his bow with him. He felt a little self conscious facing these two, casually stood with longbows as if they were scruffy models; Naomi with a fist full of arrows and Ross with his medieval waistcoat. Malcolm had heard that Ross did a bit of historical re enactment in his free time as well as the archery.

"Malcolm," Ross nodded coolly to the man. "Not shooting today?"

"No. The sights on my compound are broken. Haven't shot the spare one in months – the poundage will be far too high." He paused, catching a look go between the two archers. "I had an accident with my shoulder at work a couple of months ago, you know."

Didn't they just all know about it.

"Anyway," he stumbled forward. He knew a lot of the members thought he was an idiot, but he was not stupid enough not to notice where he wasn't appreciated. "I can rely on you two voting at the AGM this coming Wednesday?"

"AGM?" Naomi raised her eyebrows. As if she could be bothered to waste an evening going to listen to a group of petty minded male bitches complaining about the state of the politics of a small social club that was just supposed to be about fun and archery. Puffed up chickens that had failed in life. "I'm on holiday next week. I might be going somewhere."

"Not with these new travel restrictions."

"It's a big county."

"You wanting to be chairman for another run?" Ross cut in. In the unlikely event of him showing up, he certainly wouldn't vote for Malcolm.

"I think I've got a pretty good chance."

Ross smiled insincerely. "Then you needn't worry about our votes."

"Right, er…" Malcolm took a step backwards.

Naomi shook her head as she watched Malcolm falter around to go and speak to more friendly archers. "You are vicious sometimes, Ross."

"Yeah, well," Ross muttered, fitting an arrow to the bow. "I'm getting too old to be wasting what's left of my life being pleasant to arseholes like him."

"You make it sound like you haven't got long left to go."

"You never know with this new virus."

Naomi laughed.

Ross grinned. "You never know."

Richard Stilton stood at the living room window, listening to his brother with half an ear whilst watching the comings and goings of the street outside. Across the road there was a pale-bricked two storey building crammed with doors and small windows – a neat line of tarmac parking spaces in front. A small blue car, over ten years old, pulled up into one of the spaces and a woman wearing a long sleeved top with Japanese writing on the back stepped out of the driving seat. She pushed the driver's seat forward and leaned into the vehicle to pull something out.

"So I'm still not entirely sure where I stand with Emma," Ed continued, unaware that his elder brother was not giving him his full attention. "But I know she likes to go out dancing. We should go down town this evening. Accidentally bump into her."

"What does she do again?"

"She's a nurse."

The woman – he remembered her name was Naomi – was pulling a long thin case out of the car. The sun beat down; her red hair shimmering. The case was taller than she was. Naomi stood it vertically against the car whilst she locked the door. She'd been living in one of those flats ever since Ed had bought this house. He'd never been inside the block, but he still found it hard to believe that the architects had managed to cram six individual flats into the building. It looked as though it should be two semi-detached houses at most.

"I think there's salsa dancing in town tonight."

Richard rolled his eyes and turned away from the window. "You want to take me dancing?" He wasn't a natural born dancer. He could muddle his way through – he'd been force-taught during an assignment in Brazil a few years ago – but dancing wasn't something he went out of his way to do.

"Not you and me paired up. I'm after Emma."

"So I'll sit in the corner while you go on the pull."

"It might look a bit desperate. Two guys on the pull. Maybe we should take someone else."

"Instead of me? That sounds like a good idea."

"As well as. Tell you what, Naomi often goes to the salsa club. We'll tag along with her. That way, we're a group of mates off out for the night – I can detach to Emma if needs be; if not, I won't look too desperate. Great plan. I'll just give her a ring."

"Naomi?"

"No, Emma."

Richard slumped on the settee. "I thought you weren't going to look desperate," he muttered as Ed left the room to find his mobile. His brother could be worse than a giggling teenage girl at times, he reflected irritably. This hadn't really been the plan when he'd come down to visit for a few days. It had meant to be a few nights out with the lads, and a break away from his current concerns. An assignment had been postponed due to the uncertainty of changing entry rules into Japan and he had been left hanging around at home waiting to find out if the project was going to go ahead or not; and if not what he was going to do instead. Sitting at home alone thinking wasn't doing him any good, so it had felt in order that he visit his brother.

Ed reappeared a few minutes later, a little less enthusiastic than before.

"Not going?"

"Probably," he said. "She said she's worried about catching this disease. What disease? The one that they've set up travel restrictions for? It's a load of bollocks. It doesn't even have a name. I bet it doesn't exist; they're just using the rumours as an excuse to play big brother."

"Maybe," Richard said, thinking about the official line the Japanese Embassy was taking for the time being. The film that, if postponed much longer, would have to wait until next year as the season would soon be over. "But I think it's more a case that they don't know what it is yet."

"A nameless disease?" Ed didn't look impressed. "Come off it; it'll just be the flu all over again. Fuss about nothing.

We're going to the salsa tonight, and you and I are going to get lucky."

The boning in her salsa dress pinched slightly at her sides, and Naomi wondered if she hadn't put a little weight on in the last year. And with the ridiculous stockpiles of food in her flat, she wasn't going to loose it any time soon either.

Richard Stilton, sat in the bus seat in front of her, twisted around to say something to his brother, Ed, who had slung himself in next to Naomi as they'd got onto the bus into town. She wasn't completely sure what part she was supposed to be playing in this little drama planned by Ed. Apparently they – as in Ed – wanted to go to the salsa evening, but didn't want to look as though they were on the pull. Hence turning up as a group, with a woman, would improve credibility. She got the impression she may or may not end up playing fake girlfriend before the evening was at a close.

Ed lived in the semi-detached house across the road from her little flat. And whilst they were actually on sociable terms way and beyond that of most neighbours, she did not generally socialise with Ed on a regular basis. She had spoken to Richard a few times in the past as well, but she had never been out on a night with them.

They made a curious pair of brothers – Ed for city living, and Richard looking like he'd just rolled out of the great wilderness. Ed was neat and sharp – short hair, slightly spiked; shirt and jacket. Richard's hair was long and straggling down to the nape of his neck. He was in scuffed khaki trousers and a T-shirt with over shirt.

"Do you actually know how to salsa dance?" Richard was asking his sibling, his Yorkshire dialect like honey over gravel.

Ed waved off the question as unimportant. "I've been a few times. The important thing is to look as though you know what you're doing."

The way a lot of great pretenders had got to where they were now – jobs, careers, marriages, positions in the community. Half of them were no better qualified that the next to do what they did – in some cases less qualified – only that their attitude suggested otherwise.

"How about you, Richard?" Naomi asked.

"No."

"Sure he does. There was that woman in Brazil."

"Brazil?" Naomi sounded surprised. "Did you live there?"

"Worked there a couple of months."

"Richard's a cameraman," Ed added, bragging where Richard would have let the conversation finish. "I've told you haven't I? Been all over the place making natural history documentaries."

"And dancing in your free time."

He looked unimpressed. "Less glamorous than you think. Most of it's just sitting around waiting for something to happen."

"I wish I had a job with a bit of travel," Ed sighed glumly, looking out of the grimy bus window to the darkening skies. "I turned thirty last year and I've never even been outside of Europe. I wonder if I've missed chances. And he's been all over. Even been to weird places like Papa New Guinea where they eat people."

"You're a poor, hard-done-by bugger, aren't you?" Richard laughed, glancing over at Naomi who smiled as if to humour the excitable little boy in Ed. "And they don't eat people in Papa New Guinea."

"Don't know whether I could do Papa New Guinea, though," Ed mused as if it were a real possibility. "I can imagine it's a bit primitive there. Jungle folk."

"Some of them live right out in the wilds," Richard nodded. "But if someone pulled the plug, I don't suppose they'd even notice. I know who I'd give a better chance of survival."

"Will you listen to you two," Naomi cut in. "There's no call to be so maudlin." She reached forward to press the bell for the bus to halt as they approached the theatre bus stop. "We're supposed to be going out to have some fun."

"Too right," Ed said. "Let's go find Emma."

Emma and her nursing friends who were wavering over whether to come had not arrived yet. The trio got a table at the side of the club with a good view of the dance floor. Richard went to the bar, and they sat and watched the beginners' lesson end. Then the lights would be turned down a notch, the Latin atmosphere tuned up and the serious dancing would begin.

Ed looked worried. "I want to impress Emma."

"The way you were fussing on this afternoon, I'm sure she's already got the bloody message," Richard muttered good-naturedly into his beer.

"Thing is, they say women like a man who can dance," Ed continued. He paused for a moment, looking over the crowd. "Naomi," he turned to her as if just having realised there was a woman at the table. "Do you like a man who can dance?"

She shrugged. It didn't really matter. "Sure."

"I have done this before," he said, his eyes caught by a South American looking couple who were making easy work of some complicated moves. "But it's been a while. I don't want to look a complete pratt. You don't fancy going through the basics with me, Naomi?"

She smiled, amused by his obvious nerves. Ed always had this façade of being streetwise and smooth; daddy cool as he strolled out of his house to the car on a morning. Richard caught her eye. "Is this a family thing?"

"Nah. I'm the laid back one."

"Come on, Naomi; let's dance before Emma gets here."

"Looks like we're abandoning you," Naomi said to Richard as Ed dragged her from her seat. They went out into the dance floor, which was still quite empty. Ed stood in front of Naomi, holding her hand but not sure what to do.

"You do realise that the man is supposed to lead?" Naomi goaded gently.

"Ah, shit."

"You can do this." She stepped around, putting her hand on his shoulder. "You remember the beat, right? One-two-three-pause-five-six-seven-pause."

"That's it." He still didn't make a move to start.

"Okay, forward on your left to start."

Ed muddled his way through the track with Naomi. He shuffled where she danced; but she had been coming to these evenings most weeks for the last couple of years. The slanted skirts of her indigo dress swished around her legs as she stepped and turned, trying to get Ed to relax into the dance. Richard remained at the table, watching them. They made quite a smart couple – Ed in his casual suit and Naomi in a dress that looked made for dancing – a boned, fitted bodice with straps, going down to loose, light skirts.

"You don't appear to be dancing."

Richard looked around as a voice accused in his ear. A bright, smiling Spanish woman in black trousers and vest top picked up his bottle.

"You've almost drunk this," she noted, putting it down out of reach. "I think it's time to dance."

"Can't really say no, can I?"

"Certainly not."

Naomi gazed over the couples dancing, watching as Susana, the Chilean ex-pat she knew in passing from these club evenings, came onto the dance floor with Richard. They were chatting, easy as if they'd known each other a while. Not overly showy and complicated, but Ed's brother could dance his way modestly without having to put much obvious effort into it.

Naomi looked back at Ed. "You're supposed to be having fun."

"I am."

"Then why are you grimacing?"

The track slowed and faded out, the dancers pausing in the play. A cheer went up from a couple sat at a table as a requested song came out of the loud speakers.

"Mind if I cut in?"

Ed and Naomi looked across to Susana. She was a small woman, but hard to overlook, exuding personality. She religiously came to these club evenings, and was known to teach lessons when the regular instructor was sick or had to cancel.

"I teach," she added, "and someone told me you're a bit nervous."

Ed puffed out his chest a little. "I don't get nervous."

"Okay, you're not nervous. But you want a crash course." She looked to Naomi. "Do you mind?"

She shook her head. "Go for it."

As Susana and Ed danced off, Naomi's arms sank down. Her hands were picked up and she was turned around. "Sorry, that was my idea," Richard told her as she turned under his arm. "She mentioned she teaches here."

"She's very good. And I'm no teacher."

The song picked up in pace and more people came onto the dance floor. Naomi and Richard swung around into the throng. She saw Ross from her archery club stood with his back to the bar. He looked as though he had lost something. He spotted her and waved.

Emma and her friends arrived half an hour later. Young nurses out on the town, in sparkling dresses and high heeled shoes. Emma was a particularly slender young woman with curly blonde hair coming down to her shoulders. Her face had a sunny disposition. She was wearing a halter neck top with a particularly low cut, but seemed unconcerned by the looks some of the men gave her. Ed soon spotted her and Susana tactfully danced him in that direction.

Richard was stood at the bar. He watched his brother chat to Emma; her friends soon growing bored and wandering off. Emma nodded to something Ed had just said, and they went to dance. Elsewhere he saw Naomi dancing with a dark haired man in a blue shirt and jeans.

The evening went on, most people changing partners regularly. Ed refused to give Emma up to anyone. He was smitten. The later it got, the faster the salsa tracks got. Small steps, fast turns and up close body contact were becoming essential. Nearing midnight and Naomi found herself dancing with Ross again. He'd come on his own; she hadn't dared ask about his wife, but it was obvious the woman wasn't here. Naomi usually got along well with Ross, but she was starting to grow uncomfortable. Maybe it was just the alcohol or that she was tired, but it felt as though he clasped her waist a little too tightly.

"Ah, Christ, I cannae dance this quick," Ross laughed, his Glaswegian accent even broader. They spun around, pushed up against one another by the dancing hoards. Jostled and merry, Naomi decided she should stop worrying, and laughed.

Ross moved up and kissed her on the lips.

A stone sank through her inner core and she pulled away. "No."

"Naomi..."

She wriggled her hands free of his grasp and slipped through between two couples. Stumbling through to the edge of the dance floor, she spotted her shawl on the back of a chair where she had left it. Her head was starting to spin. She needed some fresh air. Jogging, worried Ross would follow her, she went past the cloakroom and out onto the street.

The sky was inky night with stars above. The coolness slipped over her skin. Richard was perched against a window sill of a building on the other side of the narrow street, his legs stuck out rigid straight. He noted Naomi's appearance, put up a hand to say hello.

She walked slowly over. "Had enough?"

"Just taking a break. How's our Edward getting on?"

"Still attached to Emma." Naomi turned and propped herself against the window sill next to Richard. "I presume Emma's the one with the blonde curls."

"That was what I was presuming," Richard nodded. "Either that or he's switched to one of her friends." He paused, wondering what had put that disturbed look on her face when she had first stepped out from the doorway. "You had enough?"

Naomi looked down at her shoes. "Probably. I might be off home soon." She could have gone in for another dance, but she didn't want to bump into Ross again. She didn't want to get tangled up in his marital issues.

A stocky man in a rugby shirt came out of the club and lit a cigarette. He took a long drag before exhaling to the sky. "You two lovebirds had enough of dancing?" he asked, walking over to them. "Dancing's not my thing either. Only came for the missus. Was dying for a fag." He looked down at the black shawl Naomi had in her hands. "You want to get that on you, love," he advised. "Don't want to be catching a cold."

She smiled weakly. "No, I suppose not." She swung the shawl around her exposed shoulders.

"Might catch that disease everyone's whispering about. The one we can't travel for."

"The nameless one?"

He laughed, "That'd be the one. They say it's like the flu."

"I think everyone's just overreacting," Naomi added.

"Yep, load of bullshit if you ask me," the man with the cigarette concurred.

"I don't know about that," Richard said, scraping at the paved street with the heel of his shoe. "I was supposed to be going to Japan to work for a couple of months, but we can't get in. They're not even letting tourists in."

"Getting tough with the visas? Well, the Japanese are panicking too."

"You don't need a visa as a tourist. Not usually. Besides, there aren't any cases in Japan. There must be something to worry about. There's rumours they're going to be closing the borders."

"What?" Naomi turned to look at him, a little aghast that he appeared to be serious.

"Japan's just islands. Easy to keep a disease out if you don't let anyone come in."

"That can't be right."

"Japanese nationals abroad have been advised to travel home in the next couple of days," Richard continued. "Of course, none of this is official, but there are rumours, and we can't get our working visas to go film there. Makes you think that someone thinks this disease is serious enough to start taking precautions."

"Yeah, and they've restricted travel here," the stranger pointed out, as if his bullshit theories were already tossed aside. Easily persuaded to take the other side of the argument; not really sure of anything.

Naomi felt uncomfortable. A nervousness that something bad this way was coming. She pulled her shawl tightly around her body. "They always make a fuss about new outbreaks. They never come to anything."

"Most of the time they don't." Richard was staring at the sky. "Doesn't mean it won't this time." He paused dramatically, then broke into a grin and nudged Naomi with his shoulder. "No point worrying. That won't change anything."

She felt her body relax. "So you were making it up about Japan?"

He shook his head. "But it doesn't mean it's the end of the world. Just that my work will be postponed till next year."

Next year. A phrase that suddenly felt a long distance from them. And no one knew how things would be at that point.

Sunday mornings. Hazy images of the previous night blurred together in a crumpled pile. A hot throng of bodies. Movement. Elbows poked into her ribs. Sharp steps; salsa heels clicking on the floor. Naomi propped herself up on her elbows in bed and gazed across her cramped bedroom. Her salsa dress was hanging on the back of the door. Limp and inert again.

She yawned, and stretched her body down the length of the mattress before checking the time on her bedside table. It was already eleven in the morning. Normally that would have depressed her twofold: she didn't like to waste her days – *her* days as opposed to work days; especially on a Sunday when work was just around the corner. But she had two weeks of holiday coming up. There would be no Monday morning blues tomorrow.

Getting out of bed, she wandered into her living room. Stepping around a stack of soup cans, she grasped the double doors in the corner of the room to reveal the kitchenette – the thought of a kitchen shoved into a cupboard. The flat was that small. Considering the diminutive dimensions, it was impressive how much the architect had squeezed in, but it was grim reality how pitifully small her space was. Switching on the kettle, she flopped onto the settee and gazed out of the window to the sunlight from her shadows.

Her mobile started ringing and she answered without bothering to check who it was.

"Hello."

"Naomi, it's Ross here."

Her stomach contracted; the sound of his voice reminding her that which had already been forgotten. Ross and his troubled marriage. She really didn't want to become a third party in that little drama. She hoped he wasn't going to try and start anything with her.

"Oh," she started, sounding less than enthusiastic.

There was a hushed pause as if he was considering his options. "I was just ringing to say sorry about last night. We're still mates, right?"

"I don't know," she replied, "That really depends…"

"Ah, come on," he complained. "It was just the drink, you know. We're having a bit of a rough patch and the drink lost my head. It didn't mean anything. You know I wouldn't go for you," he laughed awkwardly – the suggestion ludicrous. "I mean, you, Naomi…"

"All right," she interrupted sharply. "End with apologising and don't get onto insulting."

"Ah didn't mean to insult you."

"Let's just drop it."

"So you'll be at practice this week? We're still longbow buddies."

Naomi raised her eyes to the ceiling. Quit the sugar-sweetness, Ross, she thought in silence. It really doesn't suit you. "Sure."

"Look, there's Sarah back with the shopping. I'd better go. Be seeing you."

He hung up before she had chance to say goodbye. Naomi set the mobile phone on the arm of the sofa and regarded it for a moment. On the face of things, that had been the best resolution she could have hoped for. And yet there was something almost furtive about it.

The kettle clicked off as the water reached boiling point. Naomi raised her body from the sofa to go and make a cup of tea. The land line started to ring. "For god's sake," she growled at no one – for she was very alone – and reached over for the black cordless handset. "Hello?" she almost snapped into the phone.

"Naomi?" Rudi's voice sounded confused, as if he might have dialled a wrong number.

She closed her eyes and rubbed her brow. "Rudi," she said, her voice dropping a notch. Straight onto another paranoid and messed up case. "How are you today?"

"No better."

Still barking bonkers, she thought, getting up and walking into the kitchenette. "I hope you're having a relaxing weekend now." Taking a teabag from the cupboard, she dropped it into a mug and poured in the water.

"I'm calling from my office."

"You're at work? I really think you need to take a break."

"Can't take a break now. Normal rules don't apply."

She rolled her eyes. "Will you please stop being so melodramatic. I have had enough for one weekend."

"I'm not. I'm just ringing to check you're okay."

"I'm fine." Naomi tossed the teabag into the bin, pausing to think over his voice. He sounded very calm this morning. Steady, level. Normal. Resigned maybe. It wasn't encouraging.

"There's two reported cases in York."

"What? You mean this nameless disease?"

"There's no need to worry," he didn't sound as though he believed his own words. "They're securely in the hospital. But there are cases cropping up across the country. We still don't know the original source, so it's hard to predict how far this initial infection is going to spread. Christ, it's global already."

"Except for Japan."

"What?"

"Oh, just something someone was saying at salsa last night. They can't get a working visa for Japan. They said nationals had been asked to return. I'm sure that can't be right."

"The official word came out earlier this morning. They've got forty-eight hours as of yesterday to get back."

Naomi lowered her body onto the sofa. "I thought he was joking."

"Japan doesn't have any cases. And islands are always a better protection than land boundaries when it comes to halting the spread of infection. I think they're going to watch the next couple of weeks from a very safe distance to see how things work out. You can't blame them. There's a lot of island nations who haven't any reported cases yet. We're expecting similar announcements from Australia and New Zealand soon.

Iceland's put a ban on any foreigners entering the country. Ireland's in discussion with the government to set up something similar to combine them and Northern Ireland from the rest of us over here. It's a bastard that the infection is already in here; otherwise we'd be in a much stronger position."

It was a bit too much to take in all at once. Talk you'd expect in a trashy disaster movie, but not from an old friend who was sounding as though he'd gotten over his nervous breakdown. Naomi noticed that her hand was shaking slightly. She put her cup of tea down on top of a pile of trays of canned fruit. "But this is just something like the flu, right?"

Rudi didn't answer.

"Rudi?"

He sighed at the other end of the line. "I wish it was the flu. Flu we could cope with."

Her voice sounded strained. "What?"

"Look, positive thing: it's not airborne."

That was it: the positive fact? "But surely you'll be able to control it?"

"Two weeks ago, that's what we thought. We still don't know the source. It just started cropping up: London, New York, Beijing, Toronto, Washington, Brussels, Berlin, Stockholm..." he broke off. "We didn't understand how it was spread at first, or how quickly. There'll still be people out there who are carrying it and aren't in medical care."

"But when they get sick, they'll go to the doctor."

Rudi exhaled. She could imagine him shaking his head. "I want you to take care of yourself. This thing might burn itself out in a couple of weeks; it's maybe too virulent for its own good. But if that's the case, things are going to get nasty."

"You're starting to scare me."

"I wish you lived in the middle of nowhere."

Naomi squeezed her lips together. For the first time in a long time she really wished she didn't live alone.

"Try not to worry too much. We're working on an information leaflet. People need to be informed. The government shouldn't have sat on this as long as they have. The army will be distributing it tomorrow."

"The army?" Naomi broke out, incredulous.

"You'll get it tomorrow. Keep your eye on the news: the television, the radio, the Internet. I know it's scary, but the more you understand; the better. The better your chances."

The flat felt very quiet, very empty. "Rudi, I…"

"I've got to get back to work," he told her. "You've got all my numbers, right? I'll speak to you soon."

The line broke and the droning sound of nothing filled her ear. Naomi switched off the phone and stepped over to the living room. The sun washed over her little cul-de-sac road. A woman was walking her dog up the street. Normal, mediocre life. Rudi's portents of doom didn't belong here. Couldn't. Because she didn't know how they would all cope if this was really going to happen.

PART TWO
The Beginning

Without visible facts to impact on daily routine, it was difficult for most people to remain on a state of emergency for long. Monday morning was the dredges of normality – the worst that was going to happen was that people had to go back to work. People except for Naomi.

Two weeks off. To kick start her fortnight of rest, she decided she would clean the flat, starting with washing the windows down. Lying in bed listening to the radio, it was easy to have grand plans and draw up lengthy lists of chores that would get her life in order.

She got up, took a shower and ate some breakfast. Pulling on a pair of shorts and a vest top, she took a bucket out of the cupboard and went into the bathroom to fill it up in the bath – it was a lot easier than trying to angle the bucket under the tap in the kitchenette.

The radio was tuned in for company. She took the key from the kitchen drawer and unlocked the living room windows, pushing them open wide. Gazed out at the warm sunshine. This flat was always misleading; shadowed and cooled; when the curtains were drawn it was impossible to say whether the weather was good or bad.

The current song faded out as she dropped a cleaning cloth into the warm water.

"It is now nine o'clock this Monday morning and this is the news," the radio broadcaster's voice cut in. "The government announced this morning to restricting travel to city and town limits…"

Naomi looked up sharply. Had she heard that right?

"Local army posts were set up during the night and drivers will be asked to return home. The prime minister has requested that people do not panic. This is a precaution for the best of the nation."

She lowered herself onto the windowsill. Remembering something Rudi had told her the other day. Travel restricted to counties wasn't enough. They needed total lockdown.

"This comes on the back announcements from nations such as Japan and Australia who are closing down their borders to visitors. Non-nationals have been asked to leave. Japanese nationals have twenty-four hours to return to their country; Australians have five days, before the borders will be fully closed until further notice. Other countries with no reported cases are taking similar action.

"The shadow home secretary has issued a statement that this is "a melodramatic and ridiculous response to an illness that can be, and currently is, easily contained". The prime minister reiterates that this action is currently necessary to contain the situation. Britain is not the only country to have taken such measures; Germany, Italy, Canada and Holland amongst others now have a freeze on travel. The army has been drafted in to deal with control and logistics. Any foreign nationals who need to leave should report to their local army base. Transportation to the nearest airport will be arranged. Foreign nationals should call their embassy for more information.

"The cause of this response is a new illness discovered by scientists a fortnight ago. This virus has appeared in many cities worldwide; the original source unknown. Although not airborne, the disease is highly contagious, and governments are keen to control and contain before it poses a real threat. Information booklets will be distributed to all UK households during the day and citizens are asked to remain vigilant against the risk of infection.

"For the time being, all non-essential work sectors will be closed down, and staff are being sent home until further notice. Economists are calling for a change of policy in fear that this will cripple the British economy. Any compensation…"

Naomi twisted to look out of the window, switching her mind off from the radio. This was too much. It was positively surreal. The last two weeks she had laughed to herself about

Rudi's behaviour, convinced he was having a nervous breakdown. He had been right. She felt sick.

The man who lived next door to Ed Stilton was stood on his drive, hands on his meaty love handles, looking furiously at his car. There was a screech and Ed's own car appeared from the main road. It swung around onto the drive, a breath away from tearing up the side of Richard's Landrover. It jolted to a standstill and Ed burst out of the driver's door as if he was stepping into a boxing ring.

"Fucking hell!" he shouted at no one in particular, slamming the door shut.

"You got told to sod off home as well?" the neighbour asked, walking over the lawn. He looked keen to talk. As his hands dropped to his sides, Naomi could see a slight shake.

"I got to work, and they said we have to shut the office down till further notice. The government says so," Ed spat. "What the hell is it their business? All because a few people have got the bloody flu?"

The neighbour sniffed in a cocky way as if to say Ed knew nothing. "I was supposed to be visiting my sister up in Sheriff Hutton today. You know they've blocked the ring road?"

"What?"

"Didn't you hear it on the radio? No one's allowed to travel outside the city limits. You've got to stay in your home town."

"You're joking me…"

"They have road blocks up on the roundabout here on the ring road. I bet they've got them set up on every roundabout all the way around the ring road. Army lads, trucks, road blocks." He paused, stepping closer as if there was a large crowd he didn't want to panic. "Machine guns," he stage-whispered, his eyes growing large. "I bet they've got live ammunition in them as well."

Naomi turned away from the window, clasping a hand to her hand to stop a sob tumbling out. Her mind was blank, she couldn't even think why she was worried, but she had a consuming sense of dread. It shouldn't really even bother her – she was off from work the next two weeks, she had no plans of leaving York anyway, and she had more than enough food stashed in her flat to see her through the next few months. Yet there was this overwhelming feeling of terror; that something life altering was coming and there was nothing to stop it. Something bad was coming. A disease. And it didn't even have a name.

Important information about HEMO10 Virus

This leaflet contains important information: KEEP IT SAFE

Your local army post's contact details will be printed at the bottom of this leaflet.

What is this leaflet for?
The UK government have produced this leaflet in conjunction with the British Centre for Tropical Disease, the National Health Service and army. Keep this information safe. You will need it if you encounter cases of the HEMO10 Virus.

What is HEMO10 Virus?
HEMO10 Virus is a new virus that has broken out in many places worldwide.

Because this is a new virus, no one will have immunity to it. Everyone is at risk. It is therefore important that we minimise risk of spreading the disease.

How does HEMO10 spread?
The virus particles are spread through blood, bodily fluids, saliva, vomit and diarrhoea. If any of these substances from an infected person get into your system through eyes, mouth and other bodily openings, open cuts and wounds; then you will contract the disease.

What is the UK Government doing to control this outbreak?

As you will be aware, we have frozen all public movement and request that all people stay in their homes. We have set up military control nationwide and your local military post is your first port of call if you suspect that you or your family have become infected. The virus is an aggressive strain, producing symptoms in the body much faster than most known viruses. As we have no natural immunity, it is important that we make a stand to stop the spread immediately. These precautions have been put in place for your own safety.

Is there a vaccination I can have?

Not at this stage. A vaccine can be developed when the specific strain has been identified. The British Centre for Tropical Disease is working on this disease 24/7.

What can I do to protect myself?

Stay in your home and follow all rules and instructions from your local army post.

What are the symptoms?

Symptoms begin to appear 5 to 10 hours after infection. Symptoms can include headaches, nausea, reddening of the eyes, diarrhoea, bloody diarrhoea, vomiting and bloody vomiting, slurred speech leading to loss of speech, delirium and violent outbursts. These symptoms will intensify as the hours pass.

What should I do if someone I know is showing symptoms?
Contact your local army post immediately. Isolate the person if possible. The army will come and collect the patient and take them to one of our hospitals set up specifically to care for HEMO10 patients. Speed is crucial as this disease acts so quickly.

What should I do if I think I or someone I know has been infected?
Contact your local army post immediately. As above speed is crucial with this disease, and the sooner you can get medical attention, the better. The army will collect the patient and take them to one of the quarantine units set up for suspected cases. Medical staff there are waiting to care for you. You will be tested for the disease and monitored for the following forty eight hours for symptoms.

You can access this information online in a number of languages.

Your local army post contact details:

Naomi put her head in her hands. She was sitting on the staircase – a windowless passage, cool, shadowed and cut off. A direct route from her front door to her flat on the first floor.

As soon as she had heard the letterbox snap, she had hurried down the steps; the folded white piece of paper glowing in the semi-gloom. It had been printed off on a regular printer, black and white type, no glossy pictures or thought-out layout. This was a run-through of the essential facts, prepared in a rush. Whoever had given the command to distribute these had probably been hoping things would never get this bad.

It was surprising to read that people had been asked to stay in their homes. As far as she was aware, there was simply a ban on travel. She supposed it amounted to the same thing. Hide away and hope it doesn't happen.

It was an information leaflet but having read it, she felt as though she knew less than when rumours of a nameless flu had been creeping through the country. What exactly was this disease? Even after reading the description, it was hard to imagine quite what you might see. And it was so incredibly vague. So there's no immunisation programme, and special centres were being set up to take the infected. It didn't tell you how long it would be after admission that you would be able to return home. At what point did they declare you cured? Probably when they were signing the death certificate.

Perhaps this was just a dream she would wake up from soon. Complex and intricate, every eventuality covered, but it could still be a dream, couldn't it?

Walking back up to the first floor, Naomi pinned the information leaflet to her fridge door. She padded to the front window and looked out onto the street. The army jeep with boxes of information leaflets had driven away. There was no one outside. Silence. So quiet. No traffic. Everyone was probably collapsed by the letterbox, reading the information sheet, glancing at their husbands and wives, their frightened children, and wondering where this was going.

Naomi hugged herself and looked around the flat. She didn't have anyone. Being single had never really bothered her too much, but now, now she wished she was attached. Someone she could rely on to support her. Just another person her to tell her she wasn't going mad.

She felt giddy. Sick.

Picking up the telephone, she dialled her mother's number. Three rings before a reply. Naomi wondering why her mother hadn't bothered to call her only daughter yet. Was she not worried?

"Hello?"

"Hello, Mum," Naomi started, surprised by just how nervous her voice sounded.

"Naomi!" Her mother sounded particularly cheery, as if just pulled out of a garden party by the telephone. "This is a nice surprise. How are you?"

She wasn't quite sure how to respond. They did know what was happening in Scotland, didn't they? Her mother lived in a little village in the Borders. Moved up there seven years ago, claiming she was sick of England and its English ways. The fact that she herself was English didn't figure.

"Not brilliant."

"Oh dear." There was a pause. "You're not sickening for this thing everyone's getting in a tizz over, are you?"

"HEMO10 virus," she said, the name of something that had been a nameless distant threat until today. "No, of course not. I'm just frightened."

"Frightened? Goodness, there's no need for that. It's all a fuss about nothing. You know what they're like. Every time a new strain of flu breaks out the newspapers all go mad – good chance to sell copies. And it always comes to nothing. Now, dear, it's just like that. It'll soon blow over."

"This isn't exactly the flu."

"Oh, whatever it is, I'm sure we'll be fine. We got some silly leaflet through the letterbox today. I heard they're shutting the border between England and Scotland. Well, there aren't any cases in Scotland, you know."

She squeezed her eyes shut. "There are confirmed cases in York."

"Really? I hadn't heard that."

"Rudi told me."

"Rudi? Oh yes, Rudi, that funny one you used to share a flat with. Isn't he working for the NHS or someone like that nowadays?"

"Someone like that."

"Well, there you go. They're on the case. Nothing to worry about. Give it a couple of weeks and this will all have blown over. Look, darling, I was just on my way out to my knitting group. Please don't worry, it will all be fine."

Naomi felt her face crumble. Little child back with the mother who was too busy. This wasn't the reassurance she was looking for.

"I'll ring you tomorrow," her mother chimed. "Must dash."

She whispered: "Bye." Putting the phone onto the seat beside her, she stared at the wall. Now what was she supposed to do?

Pushing the coffee table out a little, she slipped down to sit on the floor. Flipped up the lid of her laptop computer and switched it on. Rudi had told her to keep informed. Maybe there would be some news, some more information about what was happening. Perhaps this was a very temporary measure and everything would be all right in a couple of days.

Riots. Violent images taken by press photographers running into the fray. Covering the story of the century. No one had anywhere to go, but they didn't want to be locked up and confined. Riots and protests. London, Bristol, Manchester, Cardiff... swollen roads with blocked arteries. The pile up of cars at the exits onto the ring road at York; trying to get out. Army roadblocks: trucks and jeeps, barbed wire, machine guns, soldiers – it looked like a war zone. A nightmare only a few hours old. Warning shots had been fired when the crowds threatened to turn nasty. The police dealing with riots in the larger cities were struggling to control the general public feeling of fury. In Cardiff someone who was infected had gone to the riot. They realised later, seeing the man and realising he wasn't well. They thought he had infected other people. There was no information how he had done this or just how he had behaved. Only that things were getting out of control.

Ireland, similar to Scotland in that it had no reported cases, was in a better position with the Irish Sea keeping it safe from the neighbouring infected island. The borders were closed. No one was allowed in. Some people on the coast of Wales had gotten into fishing boats and headed for the Emerald Isle. Already there were refugees. Begging sanctuary. The Irish government had set up a quarantine centre for refugees coming to the country.

There was just one thing on people's minds. Run. Run away. But where should they run to?

High on Skye – the Ultimate Islander's Blog

Fàilte! Or welcome. Välkommen i Skottland. Or whatever the fuck you want to say. I am the sometimes unemployed twenty something Skye resident. Raised in Portree, working when the tourists come in. Sitting on my arse through the winter. This is my life.

01 May 20--

So they blockaded the fucking bridge over to Skye. Load of bloody nancy boys, can you believe it? You'd think we'd have more sense up here than to take all this southern scare mongering seriously. What do they think is going to happen? Our lad over in Kyle of Lochalsh thinks it's really funny. Like a diseased person is going to turn up this far north. And even if they did, they'd get beaten to death. In the meantime, we've barricaded ourselves on Skye, and if there is any infection here, we've locked ourselves in with it. That's what he's saying anyway. Lucky for him that bridge is blockaded.

There's no disease on Skye. It's a pain in the arse because I was supposed to be working at the camp site at Glen Brittle this summer, but no one is going to come on holiday now. On the other hand, we won't be accidentally appearing in a million tourists' photos this year; we have the island for ourselves. No worries – we've locked ourselves in with a fucking distillery. Talisker all round, boys. Mint.

From: teresainoz@fastmail.co.uk
Sent: 01 May 20-- 12:04:35
To: naomiarcher@aceserver.co.uk

Subject: I'm coming home shocker

Hi Hun,

How are things? Bet you weren't expecting to get an email like this so soon. I've barely been over here six months and I did say I was going to do at least 2 years.

No, I haven't squandered all my cash yet. Thing is, I've been told I have to get out. I guess you'll have heard all about it over there anyway. Really weird. We've all been told (non-Aussies, I mean) that we've got 5 days to get out of the country. They won't really tell us very much; just that Australia's going to shut down its borders. Apparently a similar message has gone out worldwide to Aussie nationals telling them they've got 5 days to get home or else it's tough.

What is going on? I feel really out of touch here. I never bother watching the news. Shane said New Zealand's adopting a similar policy. Are we going to war or something?

I'm really sad to be having to leave so soon. I was just getting to know Shane, if you know what I mean? He said I should just ignore it and stay put. It won't last forever. But it's a bit scary, I mean, I've never had any official command like this. And it's Australia; they're all so chilled out here. Why are they freaking out?

I don't know how I am going to cope back in the UK. I haven't got a job or anywhere to live. I'll probably end up back with my parents. Maybe I'll have to crash with you – ha ha! In your hole of a flat.

Never mind. Be seeing you sooner that you think.

Hugs/ Teresa

From: naomiarcher@aceserver.co.uk
Sent: 02 May 20-- 05:25:06
To: teresainoz@fastmail.co.uk

Subject: Re: I'm coming home shocker

Hi Teresa,

I hope you get this – I read online that some of the UK servers may end up going down. Non-essential staff have been sent home; things are going to start falling apart. There won't be the personnel to maintain all the networks. Well, that was what they wrote in the article, but maybe they're looking at the worst case scenario.

If I were you, I'd stay put. If this blows over you'll be able to come back to the UK as originally planned, and if it doesn't… you wouldn't want to come back.

I honestly don't know what's going on but it's terrifying. They've restricted travel severely within the UK. I've heard they've similar problems in the US, France, Germany, China… etc etc… You remember Rudi? He ended up working in that weird pathology department for rare diseases. He's working on this and he is really worried. He has me stockpiling food. It's like we're preparing for the end of the world. Honestly, if someone doesn't come and physically drag you out of the country, I'd stay put.

Take care and keep in touch.
Naomi

PART THREE
Incubation

It had not been a good night for Ed. Since his short education, leaflet-supplied, on this disease, *hemodeath* or whatever they were calling it, he had been worried. Other people had been worrying long before this, but Ed didn't let the concerns of the outer world affect him if he could help it. Yesterday morning he had just been pissed with having to leave work; not being allowed to get out of the city until further notice.

Richard, who had been sat in front of the computer for bloody hours, said that he'd read an article that there were cases in the hospital in the centre of town. Where Emma worked. It was too risky; she needed to be out of there. He'd tried calling, left frequent voicemail messages and texts. She wasn't responding. He'd barely slept all night. What if she got infected?

Richard glanced up from his laptop as Ed paced back through the living room. On the mobile phone again. Perhaps he ought to take the hint that she either didn't want to or couldn't speak to him. He looked out of the window, and saw Naomi walking out of her building. What was she doing? He'd just been reading the government advice online. They suggested remaining in your home unless absolutely necessary.

"Maybe I should head down to the hospital."

"What, where all the sick people are?"

"Oh come on, they're sick, they'll be too weak to bother you after they've been shitting out their guts."

"The advice on here is to stay at home."

Ed tossed his mobile irritably onto the settee. "I don't know what the fuss is about. They said so themselves in that print out – it's not airborne. You'll only catch it by having sex with a sickie."

"I think it was any kind of bodily fluid."

"So they cough on an open cut. Just plaster up."

The question that preyed on Richard but didn't appear to present itself to anyone else was: where did the open wound come from in the first instance? Richard stared evenly at his brother. He'd spent most of the night on the internet looking at news websites from across the world. It was as if time bombs had detonated world-wide, independently and all at once. From a few instances here and there, it had exploded into outbreaks. Governments were taking extreme action to try and control the incidents before they got out of hand. In some cases it might just work; in others places they were falling into anarchy.

Ed was at the front window, glaring out at the sunshine. "Look at it out there. This is all one great big over-reaction."

"York seems to have had it easy so far," Richard commented. Even so, he wished he was at home: his house in a little village. Just ride this out in isolation. "The police were busy last night rounding up looters on Coney Street. Few attempted and a few successful rapes; more than usual they reckon."

"Rape?" Ed turned around.

"I suppose people think the police have got other things to be dealing with."

"But rape," Ed repeated.

Richard leaned back in his seat. "Come off it, Ed, you know what people are like. Nothing like a disaster to bring out the worst in the human race. You heard about the tsunami over in East Asia – all the unclaimed and orphaned kids after the sea had washed back. The sex traffickers got in there, claiming those with no where to go."

"Yes, but that's perverts and criminals."

"We're under military rule effectively. No one's supposed to be going anywhere. That's a big fucking job for the army and police to do. They're not going to have the time to deal with every incident. A lot of people will be thinking this is the time to do those things they never dared do under normal circumstances. A lot of people don't commit crime because they're afraid of getting caught; not because they think it's morally wrong."

"So we've got all out muggings and rape and pillage and you reckon York's got it easy?"

"A lot of places have rioting. It kicked off yesterday, and they haven't managed to break it up in some places still. There have been infected people in the riots. They don't always know they've got it to begin in, and there seems to be a point in which they're hell-bent on spreading the disease. Can you imagine a more perfect environment for spreading disease: an out-of-control riot?"

"But it's not airborne. What are they going to do, cough on people?"

"Don't be naïve. That leaflet said that sufferers become increasingly violent. They attack people; they bite people. Their saliva gets into your blood stream and you're infected. I've been reading a bit on this French website. They've had some really bad rioting in Paris."

"Don't you mean strikes?" Ed tried to be funny.

"They were trying to apprehend people that were obviously infected; to get them away from the general public; get them some medical care. Didn't realise just how violent people get. A few officers were bitten; and now they're out of action because they've got to be put in hospital for observation. In the early hours of this morning they took the decision to shoot to kill."

"Shoot to kill who?"

"The infected."

"What?" Ed coughed. "But they're people. Jesus. They need to be put in hospital, not killed. Our government had better not start with that kind of shit."

"What do you think they're going to do for you in hospital?"

"Make you better."

Richard shook his head. Why did people expect morality in these situations? That the great big mythological lie that it will all work out in the end will save everyone in the end. And if not everyone, then me at least – because these kinds of things only happen to people you don't know. "There's a website on here, the un-official truth about the HEMO10 virus. I think it was written by the researchers who have been studying this disease since it first cropped up. They tell it how it is."

Ed's mobile started ringing. The two men stared at the object on the sofa for a moment as if unsure of what to do. Ed marched over and picked up the mobile. "Hello," he barked. "Emma?" His face brightened and he left the room.

Richard sighed and looked down at the laptop screen. He had the impression his younger brother wasn't taking this as seriously as he ought to. Either that or Richard had been reading too much exaggeration online. But people ought to know the facts as the medical community understood the situation. Even it if was scary. People needed to be scared; to fully appreciate just how dangerous things might become.

He flicked over to the UK news website, and raised his eyebrows when he saw that the current headlines had just been displaced by breaking news. "Irish Massacre." That wasn't good news: as far as he was aware, there weren't any cases confirmed in Ireland.

He read through the article, feeling sick. Not that you could blame them. The longer this went on, the more self-preservation would become the reigning rule of decision making. We'd all be alone in this nightmare soon. For wasn't it true that every man dies alone?

Ireland had quickly set up a quarantine centre on the west coast for refugees sailing over from the Welsh coast; a few from the English coastline intermingled. Ireland had already closed its borders to the world and said that no one was welcome. But still these frightened people got in their fishing boats and sailed for sanctuary. Considering the news and pictures that were coming out of countries where the infection was becoming rife, they couldn't send these people back to die. A compromise had been quickly reached. The incomers would spend a week in the quarantine, and when it was clear that they were not infected – there wasn't enough common knowledge shared across the board on how to identify this new disease in blood samples – they would be allowed to come out into Ireland.

That had been the plan. It would have worked, if one family had not lied about the bandage on a young daughter's arm. They were too terrified to admit to themselves or the authorities what had happened. Close your eyes and hope it goes away. Besides, they probably didn't understand exactly what this virus was. They had probably just hoped their daughter would sweat it out.

In the early morning, the young girl had woken showing signs of hysteria and rage. She had bitten her mother. Other people in the holding pen had woken to see the mother; a thin trail of blood winding down her neck. The girl ran for a young boy and bit him on the face. His parents threw the girl off their screaming son. Blood, panic. People rushed at the locked doors. No one managed to restrain the little girl properly; always in biting distance.

The men with the task of watching over the refuges watched in horror as the group descended into anarchy. It was like watching a rabid pack of dogs. From what they had been told, they had come to understand it as a wasting disease: bloody diarrhoea and vomiting. A person would be soon dehydrated and weak. Easily dealt with.

This was a country with no cases. Free of disease. Out of charity they had unknowingly invited it into the country. They had been told that under no circumstances was this disease to get out into the population, should it come over on the ships. They had opened fire on the people in the holding pen. Unable to tell who was infected and who was still unhurt, they had killed everyone. Announcements were sent back that no one was welcome. Boats would be told to turn around and go home. If they persisted on approaching, they would be attacked.

Ed came back into the living room. "That was Emma," he told Richard. "She's just starting a long shift at the hospital. I told her to quit the place and get up here."

Richard shut the article on Ireland. "Has she seen anyone with it?"

"Yeah," Ed sighed. "They've got about twenty of them in there."

"Twenty!"

"They're all heavily sedated. That's all they've been told to do with them. Keep them sedated; don't let them wake up. We'll let you know when we've got something more. None of the antiviral stuff has any effect on it. She said they all start leaking… you know, blood, shit and that. And the people who go and clean them up have to be in full biohazard gear."

"Jesus."

"They've already taken one out in a body bag."

Richard put the laptop lid down. "This is really bad."

"You're telling me. I bet you're wishing you'd never come to visit. You'd be much better off out of the way of people."

From: teresathekoala@noworriesnet.com.au
Sent: 02 May 20-- 10:40:06
To: naomiarcher@aceserver.co.uk

Subject: Please don't junk this Naomi!

Naomi,

How crap is this? Noworriesnet? Not that they are loving their stereotypes. I really hope your email doesn't file this as junk.

My fastmail account isn't working. Not sure why. So I had to give up and get something new.

I'm going to stay put. I got an email from my brother yesterday – he lives in London, you know – and things sound so scary. What the hell is going on there? And if you say that guy Rudi is freaking out… God, I am so worried about you.

I spoke to this woman at the British embassy over here. They're not leaving. Australia is having a total lockdown on its borders on the 06 May. As it is, they're only letting nationals in, and they're getting put in some kind of isolated quarantine. There's rumours they may bring the deadline forward. Officially everyone is supposed to go home. But if your visas are still valid, they'll honour them. She said we're better off staying here because there have been no reported cases in Australia. No reported cases.

I've started watching the news, although it doesn't tell you much. Just some sort of contagious virus is cropping up across the world. I suppose they don't want to start a panic. But they say it's fatal. I saw there has been a sudden bloom of reported cases across England and Wales. Ireland's not got any yet and Scotland is terrified. They've got the army patrolling the border. The news here is more internationally focused. Are there any cases in York? I hope it misses out the north of

England. You're not so heavily populated. Anyway, this has to be the usual media hysteria, right?

Keep in touch. I am really worried about you guys. Teresa

When Naomi got up that morning and checked her email, there was just one message in her inbox, from a friend in Australia. She downloaded the email, thought about replying, then switched off her computer. She didn't know what to write.

Outside it looked so blissfully beautiful. And intensely quite. There was nothing wrong with the world. The leaflet she had pinned on the fridge; the sites she had looked on the Internet last night: they were all just words. It couldn't be as bad as all that. The media always made a drama of the slightest thing. Her mother certainly wasn't concerned in the slightest. Maybe she was just overreacting. She stood at the window and looked outside. She needed to get out of the flat.

Pulling on her shoes, she took her keys from the bookshelf and jogged down the staircase. She put her hand on the door as if testing for heat. Took a deep breath and unlocked the door.

There was no one out on the street. The roads were silent – what with no one being allowed to leave the city, there wouldn't be much point in driving anywhere. They hadn't been told that they had to stay indoors, but with no work and no travel, most people wouldn't feel as though they had anywhere else to go, she reasoned. Most people had homes that felt larger than a shoebox with a couple of holes kicked in the side that an estate agent might call windows.

It was a little eerie walking through the streets to the little church by the river. As if life had ceased to exist; only Naomi remained to suggest the human race had ever walked the earth. She couldn't help but glance over her shoulder, half expecting to see someone dive behind a lamppost, not quite quick enough. There was no one there.

She turned off the main road and up the old village road – now just a back track where a village north of York had originally been before rapid building spread out and the outlying farming villages were sucked into the overall body of the city. Someone had a radio playing.

Naomi headed down a single-lane track, over a small stone arch bridge giving passage over the narrow, slow moving river. Up ahead was the old church. A neat graveyard circling around, enclosed by stone walls. In front there was a modest car park for church goers and walkers.

Her footsteps crunched on the gravel as she passed through the entrance gap in the wall, and moved into the graveyard. She followed the flagstone path up and around the church. The doors looked to be locked. Nothing here. Behind the church, it was shadowed, cooler. Naomi paused and scanned over the graveyard. Whenever she took this walk, she usually bumped into at least one dog walker. Gravestones sticking up; smooth arches, crosses and square tops. Maybe someone could crouch down and hide behind a stone.

She hurried away, up the path away from the church. It soon connected to a dusty farm track, running level with the river, a field separating them. Here there was no shelter, and the sun battered down. She stuck her hands in her trouser pockets and ambled up the road. She passed by a couple of fields before she remembered that this route took her over the ring road and further north to the next bridge over the river.

The ring road was said to be controlled by road blocks and army posts to keep people from leaving the city. The farm track rolled down to meet the tarmac expanse of the York ring road; strangely silent of traffic. She stood on the edge and looked one way then the next. Maybe she shouldn't have come out.

Part of her wanted to cross the ring road – just because she could although she wasn't permitted. It wasn't as though she was going to leave the city and flee. She was just going for a walk. Never the less, she ran across the road and hurried up the ascending track onto the other side.

The path went up between a hedge and a field full of growing crops. She wondered if farmers came under the grouping "essential personnel" and would be allowed to continue with their work. She supposed they must be: everyone still had to eat. She couldn't imagine there were army posts set up in the little hamlets and far flung farms to keep an eye on people's movements. They would be free to roam through the countryside as they wished. What she would have given to be living somewhere out of the way.

At the top of the field there was a wide metal bar gate. Beyond that a rutted track edged by high hedges. The track went all the way up into the village Haxby, just north of York. This track was an access route for the water board – she thought they had a small building up here somewhere.

She walked up the track for a few minutes until she reached the gap in the hedge on her right. Here there was a footpath leading back down to the river by the edge of a field. She turned off the track and towards the water.

About half way between the hedge and the river, Naomi slowed to a concerned halt. She was certain she could hear something out of place. She turned and looked back up to the track.

There was a dishellveled man stood in the gap of the hedge. He had a baggy T-shirt and shapeless trousers on. His breathing was heavy, raspy – it was what had alerted her to the fact she was no longer alone. She might have just presumed him a jogger and moved on, but there didn't seem to be anyone apart from herself who was mad enough to go for a stroll today.

The man made a sound and took a couple of awkward steps forward.

A look of concern crossed her face. His arm was shaking and there was something dripping from his fingers. He didn't look well. "Are you all right?" she called out. "Have you been in an accident?"

This contact seemed to snap the man out of his daze. He picked up his feet and began to stagger down the footpath towards her with increasing speed. He never said a word.

As he neared, Naomi could see there was quite a nasty wound on his neck; soft and moist, sparkling in the sun. The shoulder of his T shirt was stained with blood; it was probably blood that was dripping from his fingers, a trail running back up the footpath. Blood seeping into the earth.

He started to make a kind of growling sound, his mouth opening and his lips stretching aggressively back across his teeth. His red-rimmed teeth. His gaze suggested he wasn't all there.

Naomi could feel her fingers shaking. This wasn't right. Without any conscious effort or decision, she found herself glancing around for something to defend herself with. "Just steady back there," she called out to him. She spotted a branch lying in the grass just off to her right. She took a couple of back steps towards the river, leaning across to pick up the branch.

He was only a few meters away. His eyes looked angry, dark, bloodshot. He was flexing his fingers. He cried out and broke into a full run. Naomi felt her heart jump to hide up in the base of her throat. "Stay away!" she shouted at the stranger, swinging the branch up over her shoulder. She jogged backwards a few metres, hoping her threatening stance would put him off. If anything, it only seemed to encourage him.

He flew at her and Naomi swung her weapon around, smacking him heavily in the shoulder and knocking him off his feet. She nimbly danced backwards as the man tottered and dropped onto his hands and knees in the grass, making a low groaning noise. He wobbled about in his place, his head brushing the blades of grass like a primitive kind of cow.

The air pulled heavily into her lungs. Naomi swung the branch back up over her shoulders like a golf club. Ready for round two. She felt sick. The man shuffled on the ground. Oh Christ; she panicked; what if he had just been in a traffic accident and was dazed. She'd just walloped an injured man. She didn't know what to do now.

"Are you all right?" she whispered.

The man made a guttural sound and looked up. As if he hadn't realised she was there. He looked at her and hissed like a cat, baring his teeth. Then he was rustling across to her on all fours, grabbing out with dirty stained fingers.

Archery is a sport that particularly relies on the shoulder and arm muscles. In fact, it was said that the old graves of English longbow archers could be picked out from the overdeveloped shoulders of the skeletons. Naomi hadn't reached that state, but she had a good arm and a powerful swing. There was an awful crack as the branch met the side of his head. Blood splattered up her trouser leg. A contorted look of pain wrinkled its way into his face as his body was flung into the wild grass and brambles by the hedgerow.

Her knees were literally starting to shake, as if they were ready to pull apart. The man lay still. He didn't make anymore growling sounds; it didn't even sound as though he was breathing. "Oh Christ," she whimpered, looking desperately around the field. The branch dropped limply from her hands. She had killed him. She had just killed a man. And he probably just had been in a car crash, stumbling away in confusion, suffering from concussion. He had probably been crawling for help.

Probably.

It was the logical explanation, but deep down Naomi had felt like prey.

She was going to pass out. She turned away from the bloodied man and fled towards the river. The still air picked up into a breeze with her speed, rushing past her ears, whipping the hair off her face. She stumbled around the corner onto the river side path, leaning forward, gasping and retching, her hands on her thighs. She looked back to the field. She could just see the form of the man, still slumped in the grass.

"Oh no," she cried to no one.

A metallic sound, like a pan falling out of a cupboard caught her attention. There was a couple on the other side of the river, facing away from York. Mid forties, he with a black eye, both with heavy rucksacks strapped securely onto their backs. There was a pan and a metal bowl tied onto the back of the woman's rucksack. The strangers stopped and started at one another from opposite sides of the river; hostile, terrified, curious.

Naomi took a couple of steps forward, so relieved to see normal people. "Please."

The woman jumped and clutched the man's arm. They hurried along their path, dust clouding up from their hiking boots.

Pained, she watched them go. She must look to them as the man had seemed to her. But she had spoken; she wasn't aggressive. Why did they run? She looked down at herself and saw the blood splatters up her trousers. Maybe they thought she had murdered someone.

Again, she looked up to the field where the man was, and she thought she saw a movement. She panicked. Maybe he was an injured man in desperate need of medical attention, but she couldn't think. There was only one think in her head, screaming at her to run.

She sprinted down the river back towards the church. She was no athletic runner, and was soon out of breath, the blood pumping through her body, the sound of her heart vibrating in her eyes. Where the river and the ring road crossed, there was a road bridge with the river and paths going under. Naomi delved into the shadow, the change in temperature cooling the sweat on her forehead for a moment before she was back out into the full heat of the sun. She could feel her hair sticking to the sides of her face with sweat. Her face felt as though it was burning; it was probably bright red. She didn't care. She just wanted to get home. Lock the door, hide and hope this had not happened.

She jogged down a grassy track between the river and a pretty line of hedgerows. Birds twittered from the safety of branches. A water vole plopped into the river waters, scared by the approaching thud-thud of jogging steps.

Ahead was the field and then the church car park. Naomi pushed her way through the small kissing gate and over the field. Staggering over the style, she dropped into the car park, breathing so fast she might just collapse in the dust. For the first time she dared to look back the way she had come. There was no one following.

Naomi ran back out into civilised residential streets still empty of people. She jogged home, conscious of the occasional curtain twitch. People saw her and maybe they saw what she had seen in that man. She was not like that man. There had been something very wrong with him. Something not natural.

She ran down the road and swung onto her turning. The sun was still shining; her small block of flats was still there. Here normality existed. Ed's neighbour was outside washing his car; a little river of water and bubbles going down the drive to the road. Ed's garage door was up, as was the bonnet on Richard's Landrover. Neither brother was out the front. Further down the road a gangly man was walking along the footpath.

Naomi stopped in the middle of the road and looked around. She didn't know what to do. Her mind went blank. The neighbour heard her and turned away from his car, wet cloth still in hand. A look of confusion crossed his face as he saw the blood on her trouser leg. "Are you all right?" He called out to her.

She stared at him and tried to catch her breath. He took a couple of steps, down onto the pavement, then stopped. It was meeting the man in the hedgerow all over again. Except this time she wasn't speaking. She was the one breathing heavily; looking dazed.

"I've..." she started, feeling she had to say something, to let him know there was nothing to fear. "I've just been attacked."

"Attacked?" The man looked at the blood on her trousers, her dishevelled state and wondered what exactly she meant by the word attack. "We'd better call the police." He turned to go back to his house to telephone, and bumped into the thin man Naomi had seen walking up the street. The man grabbed onto the neighbour's shoulders and sank his teeth into the corner of the man's neck as if giving a particularly nasty love bite.

Naomi screamed.

The neighbour struggled with his attacker, the wet rag flailing through the air. Blood gushed down his back; arms and legs flapping ineffectually. The stranger pulled his head back, tearing a chunk of flesh away. Naomi stared as he visibly swallowed. The neighbour screamed, clutching his neck, thick dark blood pumping out between his fingers. The stranger looked at Naomi.

Oh no. She couldn't do this again. She couldn't fight again. The stuffing was knocked out of her. She felt herself whimpering, collapsing as the stranger with bloodied teeth ran at her. She had nothing to defend herself with. She was going to be torn to shreds. She started to drop to the ground.

She felt his shadow come over her, then there was a dull thack. Naomi cried out, convinced she was dying. Balled up, hunched over, not daring to look at anything. Her whole body was shaking. A repetitive serious of slapping noises echoed around her. "Don't move!" someone shouted. Thack. Naomi covered her ears. Thack.

The hitting sounds stopped. Footsteps. She was ready to gag, roll over and die. The sudden shock of cold water made her gasp; a wave thrashing over her from behind, finished as soon as it had begun, drenching her. The colour of the tarmac around her darkened, deepened with the moisture. Her thoughts were lost and she was caught up in a bubble. Rushing noises and sights. She wasn't in control of her body.

Hands grasped her head firmly, making her jolt. Lifting her gaze up from the ground. Richard Stilton was staring at her, making shapes with his mouth. He looked as white as a sheet. Rushing noise and she was pushed out of the surface of the water.

"You're going to be all right," he was telling her. His voice was so serious it was frightening. Her arms were shaking. "You are not going to die." It was a command.

"Ed?" Richard shouted, making Naomi jump with the sudden increase of volume. He stood up, pulling Naomi onto her feet with him. His hands were gripping her arms as if she couldn't stand on her own. Or to stop her from running. Bedraggled, she dared to look around. Near the car the fat neighbour was lying on his side away from her, a pool of blood around his head following the tracks of the car wash water. His body jerked randomly.

Oh god.

Moving slowly across there was a bloodied cricket bat discarded on the pavement. A human figure lying in the road, the head beyond human recognition.

Her throat contracted. She was going to throw up.

Ed came out of the front door and saw the carnage. "Fuck," he swore.

Richard seemed to be the only one who was thinking. "There's going to be another army patrol by any time now."

"How the hell do you know that?"

He didn't have time for this. "They come at regular intervals: two hours."

Ed looked at the bodies, and over to Naomi – drenched and shaking; Richard, blood splatters across his sweater as if he were a chainsaw massacre. "You two are infected."

Naomi felt Richard's fingers dig into her arms. "We're not infected," he told his brother sternly. "I didn't get any blood in my mouth or eyes. Naomi's washed off."

"The army are going to take you to one of those quarantine places. The hospitals."

The places where no one was coming out alive. Richard was shaking his head. "We're not infected. We'll quarantine ourselves if you want, but I am not going anywhere with the army." He looked around, at the puddle, Naomi dripping water. "Ed, go get your wheelie bin."

He looked bewildered, but did as he was told.

"Naomi, you have to get your shoes off."

This didn't make sense. "What?"

"You are dripping all over the place. We can't have a trail going back to your flat. The army can't know." He looked down at her shoes, her trousers. There were blood splatters. The strange thin man had only drooled a little blood onto her back before Richard had hit him out of the way with the cricket bat. These stains were something else. "Are you already injured?"

"No," she groaned. "I was attacked at the river. It's not my blood."

Ed ran across the lawn pulling his black wheelie bin behind him. "Is that my cricket bat?" he wined as he reached them. "You two have got blood stains. You're infected."

"Clothes maybe, but we're not." Richard pulled his sweater off and threw it into the bin. "It has to get into your system. You looked at that site." He turned to Naomi. "Get your shoes off," he told her. Her shoes were blood splattered. They needed throwing away; there was no point taking risks.

"She should get her trousers off as well," Ed added as Naomi was pulling off her first shoe.

"I am not stripping off in the street!"

"Your trousers are covered in blood."

"The patrol's going to be here any minute."

Your local army post, she thought. If you suspected you might be infected, you were supposed to contact your local army post. They would collect you and take you to a quarantine centre. Where all the diseased people were. That would be the end. Her trousers were covered in blood. The sensible thing to do was think of the community; follow the rules and hand yourself in. She didn't want to die. She started to take off her trousers.

"Get the Landrover's bonnet down, the bin in the garage and the garage locked. Get in your house and lock everything up," Richard was telling his brother.

Naomi threw her trousers into the bin then remembered her keys were in the pocket. "My keys," she cried out, leaning over and scrabbling for the pocket. Getting her keys, she hurried across the road to her door in only her top and knickers. Her hands were shaking so badly she couldn't get the key into the keyhole. Tears filled up in her eyes. They were going to come and take her away.

"Calm down." Richard took the keys and unlocked the door. The doorway opened and she threw herself onto the stairs, into the shadows. She thought she could hear the sound of a moving car. The army were coming to get her. They were going to take her away.

From: teresathekoala@noworriesnet.com.au
Sent: 02 May 20-- 12:35:17
To: naomiarcher@aceserver.co.uk

Subject: Emails every day

Naomi,

An afterthought. Could you email me once a day? I just find it reassuring to get an email everyday. I haven't heard from my brother since his last email and I can't get an answer on his phone. You don't have to write much, just let me know you're ok.

Thanks
Teresa

From: mailclient@noworriesnet.com.au
Sent: 02 May 20—13:00:06
To: teresathekoala@noworriesnet.com.au

Subject: Undeliverable mail

Your message entitled < Subject: Emails every day> has been returned undelivered.

Unknown domain: aceserver.co.uk

Richard stood at the side of Naomi's living room window and watched the proceedings on the street. An army patrol jeep with four men had pulled up. There was one man in the back of the vehicle, his gun ready, watching for danger. All four looked tense, expectant. It made him wonder what they had already seen in other parts of the city.

"You have blood on your leg."

He looked down and saw the splatters on his trousers. These would have to be trashed. He'd ring Ed later and get him to run across with some clothes. His gaze moved up and over to Naomi and he saw her flat properly for the first time. She was packed out with boxes and trays of food; countless cans and packets, bottles, preserves. Supplies for months. He looked back at the nervous woman. The woman who had given the impression the other night she thought this was all nonsense. "You knew this was coming."

Naomi brushed her wet hair back off her forehead. "I have a friend," she told him. "He works at The British Centre for Tropical Disease. He had me start stockpiling a couple of weeks ago."

"Shit," Richard cursed angrily. "Right when it first cropped up. They knew then how bad it was going to be and they did nothing."

She felt as though he was accusing her. "Are we going to die?"

His expression softened a little. "No. It needs to enter your system, through a cut, or your mouth or … something." She didn't look convinced. "You read the information. Five to ten hours and the first symptoms appear. We'll stay here tonight and if we're all right tomorrow morning we've nothing to worry about."

"What if one of us has it?"

Then one will have to kill the other. He didn't say it out loud. "It'll be fine. Maybe you should go get a shower. In case there's any blood in your hair or anything."

"Yes," she mumbled. "I'll go get a shower." She paused by a tall stack of trays of cans. She patted the top level. "Please help yourself to pineapple chunks."

Richard looked back to the street. One of the soldiers was speaking into a radio handset. The others looked worried. He put the handset back and said something to his comrades. There was a quick nod, then they got back into the jeep and drove away. They hadn't touched the bodies.

It was when she had gone into the bathroom and looked herself in the mirror that the nausea came on; fast and sudden, lurching up her throat. She swung around to the toilet and wretched. Her hands started to shake. She had come that close to dying; she could have been there in the middle of the road with Ed's neighbour; a slab of flesh bitten out of her throat.

She flushed the toilet and washed her hands. She hadn't been bitten or clawed. But blood had splattered and what if a drop had gotten into her system by some means? She stripped off, checking her body in a frenzy for the slightest of paper cuts or scratches. She couldn't see anything, but that was no guarantee. She wouldn't know until tomorrow morning. She got in the shower and scrubbed herself as if she would never be cleaned again.

Ed had nipped across the road with some fresh clothes when the army had driven away. The brothers had a short conversation on the doorstep, then Richard returned to Naomi's flat. He said he was sure that neither of them was infected, but that they ought to quarantine themselves just in case.

Whilst Richard was in the shower Naomi tried to check her emails. She had saved one from a friend in Australia that she meant to reply to, but the Internet kept timing out and would not connect.

Putting the laptop computer on the coffee table, she curled up in the corner of the settee and checked her messages on her mobile. Two texts: one from Ross wanting to know if she was all right; one from Rudi telling her to go and look at a website. Not much use.

She had almost died today. She might die yet of this disease. And when she stopped thinking about the virus, she realised that she might have killed someone by the river. He might have had the disease, maybe he had just been in an accident, but either way he was a person, and killing him was murder.

Naomi got up and walked to the living room window. The bodies were still lying in the street. No one was talking a walk or washing the car now.

"The army not cleared that up yet?"

She turned. Richard was stood in the doorway in the fresh clothes Ed had brought. His hair was wet from the shower. Decontaminated.

"You did that to that man?"

He moved around the boxes of food to the window. "Yeah," he sighed, surprised how easy it had come to him when he'd started. "Self defence." He looked over at her. "You wouldn't be stood here if I'd stayed in the garage."

She lowered her eyes. He made her feel guilty that she had thought of the word murder.

"You worried you're stuck in the house with a murderer?"

"Oh no," she shook her head; perhaps a little more vigorously than necessary. "Besides, if I am; then you are too."

"You're not going to tell me you've killed someone?"

"This morning I went for a walk by the river…"

"You went for a walk?" he interrupted. What did she think was happening? She must have realised how serious things were. They were under effective military rule. "Do you not read the news?"

She had always been a bit out of touch and socially stupid. She should have known. She pointed feebly at the fridge as if it were responsible. "It didn't say you couldn't go out. I knew there was a new ban on travel."

She looked about ready to cry – hardly a defence for stupidity, but he doubted this was the time to bring the subject up. "All right; you didn't know. So what happened at the river?"

"This man came at me. I tried talking to him but he didn't seem to understand me. He had a wound; there was a lot of blood. I remember him growling."

"So what happened?"

"I hit him round the head with a branch. Knocked him silly."

Slightly more effective than her response in the street, he thought to himself.

"Then I ran." She gazed out of the window. "But whether he was sick or just drunk, I shouldn't have done it. Whatever way, it's still murder."

"If you kill a person, it's murder," Richard said thoughtfully. "But if you killed an animal, it'd be animal cruelty, or self defence, or maybe even a mercy killing, depending on circumstance. Where do you draw the line between people and animals?"

She shook her head. "Don't get philosophical on me."

"What about self defence?"

"I suppose." She wandered back into the living room. "I can't help but worry that we're being irresponsible; not reporting this to the army post. If we are infected, surely we want treatment as soon as possible, to help us fight this virus. It doesn't sound very nice – vomiting and diarrhoea. Like some kind of winter flu virus, extreme style."

Richard looked at her sadly. "I think there's a website you need to see."

"A website?" Strange, he was the second person to advise this. "I tried to connect earlier but my Internet connection doesn't seem to be working. Besides, it hardly seems the time for surfing the net..." she faltered out, thinking about what she had done last night. Searching through news articles, blogs and commentaries from normal everyday people. Just needing to know she wasn't alone.

"There's a lot of stuff on the net all ready." Richard knelt down at the coffee table and turned the laptop around. "You can connect through my mobile," he added, taking the device from his pocket.

Naomi wasn't really interested in gizmos for the sake of the latest technology, and had only begrudgingly bought a basic model mobile phone a couple of years ago. Richard's looked like it was ready to replace all the electrical appliances in a modern home. "What do you do for a living again?"

"I'm a camera man," he answered as he typed something into the computer. "I get dumped in all kinds of out-of-the-way places. You'd be surprised at where technology still works. What you end up relying on for your work. Here it is."

Naomi leant forward to look at the screen. It looked like the address Rudi had sent her in a text message. "I think my friend told me to look at this."

"The one who told you to stockpile?"

She nodded. "He works for the British Centre for Tropical Disease."

"I think you mentioned that. This site is a leak from the health care professionals working with the disease. Things you need to know. It's scary but I think people should understand exactly what's going on."

"Rather than strolling by the river."

"Come on, I'm not getting at you. It's not easy to acknowledge something like this. It's like something off the bloody sci-fi channel."

"I'd better give it a read then."

The un-official guide to the HEMO10 virus

Yesterday the government released an information leaflet distributed by the army to all homes in the UK. We have read this leaflet, and feel that it is a misleading and watered-down version of what is actually happening.

The government do not want you to panic. For many that is already too late. Some have seen what this virus really does to the human body. Everybody needs to understand exactly what happens to a person when they are infected. We want you to be scared. You need to be, because if we don't all pull together and work against the spread of this disease, it will be the end. You need to appreciate just how important it is that you don't get infected.

What is the HEMO10 Virus?
This is a completely new disease. We do not fully understand it yet. There is no vaccine and no cure. We do not know where it originated from, which makes it even more important that it is isolated and destroyed as soon as possible.

It is a violent and aggressive virus. It is a hemorrhagic fever: this means blood loss in layman terms. It works far more quickly that most viruses, including virulent types such as the Ebola Virus, Borna Virus and Marburg disease virus – three virus which it shares a few traits with.

How does HEMO10 spread?
The government leaflet tells us:
The virus particles are spread through blood, bodily fluids, saliva, vomit and diarrhoea. If any of these

substances from an infected person get into your system through eyes, mouth and other bodily orifices, open cuts and wounds; you will contract the disease.

Whilst this is all correct, it may make you complacent. Please consider how easily this will work – if someone spits in your eye: you are infected. The most common method of infection we have had reported to date are as follows:
1. Prior to signs of symptoms: kissing
2. After signs of symptoms: biting

What are the symptoms?

5 to 10 hours after infection, the following symptoms will appear and will continue to intensify until death (occurring between 3 and 10 days later):

1. Headaches, paranoia, slurred speech leading to loss of speech.
2. Fever and nausea – following by vomiting, including blood.
3. Haemorrhage of sclerotic arterioles: i.e. reddening of the eyes.
4. Petechia – red or purple spots on body.
5. Hypovolemic shock – i.e. decrease in blood volume; coupled with increasing hunger.
6. Diarrhoea and bloody diarrhoea.
7. Delirium, violent outbursts in increasing frequency; psychotic and psychopathic tendencies. This is seen to culminate with the increased hunger in a single-minded "hunt, kill, eat" behaviour pattern. Cannibalism is not uncommon.
8. Cell death leading to major haemorrhaging and multi-organ dysfunction. Upon death, the abdomen will explode, spreading infected blood and decomposing body tissue across a surprisingly wide area.

What should I do if I or someone I know has been infected?

Immediate isolation. Official government instruction is to contact your local army post for collection. We can not tell you what to do. We can only point out the following facts:

1. There is no cure or treatment.
2. The mortality rate is 100%.
3. Euthanasia is illegal in the UK.
4. Murder is illegal in the UK.
5. Manslaughter on the grounds of self defence may well be a grey zone, especially in the current medical climate and military control.
6. When the infection fully takes hold, your nearest and dearest will loose their minds. They will not recognise you and they will attack. This is an aggressive virus that kills its hosts relatively quickly, so it needs to jump to its next host fast. This is the weak point we have to take advantage of if we are going to stop this disease.

Disclaimer: We are not promoting murder or euthanasia. We are not **telling** people to take the law and/or the isolation and destruction of disease into their own hands.

It was a long night.

Naomi read through the website several times. She looked at some of the news websites Richard had talked about, before she started to feel nauseous and switched off the computer. Already there were pictures posted of people suffering from the disease. Descriptions of their agony. Her body shook when she through that this might be coming to them soon. Richard was unconcerned and quite convinced he and Naomi were not infected. Naomi had a niggling doubt. Just let it be this time tomorrow so they would know for definite how it was to be.

Richard would stand at the window in shifts through the night. Watch the army come by and clear up the bodies. Watch a group of young men – really only teenagers – run up the road whooping and laughing. Throwing stones through a window. Jumping on cars. Ineffectively trying to break into one vehicle until the police arrived and took them away.

By the window was her longbow case, propped up like a slouching figure. A couple of arrows she was half way through making were set on top of some boxes.

Richard glanced across at Naomi in the artificial light. It was a side to her he had not expected. "You into archery?"

She looked dazed. It was three in the morning. The light was sleep-inducing. They had only switched on a couple of side lamps – not the main ceiling light. As if this was the war. As if you didn't want to send out signals to the enemy. "I am," she confirmed.

He looked back at the bow case. "Big bow there."

"It's a longbow. Traditional English longbow."

"No sights or anything?"

She shook her head.

"Must require a bit of technique." He drifted off, watching her. She was curled up at one end of the settee, a blanket over her feet. She looked as though she wanted to sleep, but didn't dare. "I don't mind if you want to go to bed. You don't have to stay up for me."

"I doubt I could sleep."

"Yeah," he sighed. "Everyone will be easier tomorrow."

"You seem pretty calm already."

"Do I?" he looked surprised by her observation. Weaved through the clutter and sat down next to her. "I suppose worrying'll do nowt. I don't think either of us is infected. Anyway, things have a way of working themselves out."

"You must have been in worse situations."

Richard laughed out loud, not unkindly. "I don't think I've seen anything worse than this."

"Well, no, maybe that's an exaggeration," she smiled wistfully. "But Ed was saying you've been all over the place. Didn't he say you'd even been in Papua New Guinea?" She looked at him wide-eyed. "Did things never seem desperate?"

"Ed likes to dramatise," Richard told her. "Things were never desperate. Sure, problems come up; unforeseen circumstances. You just figure out a solution and get on with it. New Guinea was good. You could honestly think the civilised world had stopped existing when you were out there. It wasn't smooth riding. Vehicles got stuck; equipment broke down. Tents got flooded out. Oh, I remember when we had a bought of intestinal worms going round the team…"

"Worms?"

"Aye, worms, in your gut. Parasites. When you went for a shit…" he faltered, catching a look on her face. Wrong company for that conversation. "You don't need to know the details. But we had pills for that. Killed off everything. Didn't feel too grand for a couple of days either myself. But we got through it."

"Hmmm," she muttered. "Except we don't have a pill for this one."

"People are surprisingly resilient. You don't know what you're capable of until you have to."

Naomi stared across the room in half light. She wasn't convinced, but she was feeling calmer. His attitude was catching. "You must be regretting coming to visit Ed when you did."

"Yeah," Richard gave a short laugh. "Although it could be worse. York's not had it too bad yet. And Ed's probably glad of the company. I don't think he'd cope that well on his own."

On your own. Some people didn't have a choice. Still, at least Rudi had prepared her well. "Didn't Ed tell me ages ago that you live in a really little village out in the Wolds?"

"That's right?"

"And your partner makes artistic ceramics."

"What, Anna?"

"I don't think he ever mentioned her name."

"Well, your information is a bit out of date, but you've got the gist of it. She moved up to Yarm well over a year ago." He shrugged; he wasn't particularly bothered about Anna anymore. "The location is good though. Pretty isolated – the village is in this valley down little back lanes. You could be reasonably self sufficient there."

"So why don't you just make a break for it?"

"What, escape back home?" He shook his head. "They've got all the roads out of town blocked. Besides, have you seen the local websites? There's jams of traffic. Everyone's panicking and trying to get out. Getting no where." He paused, looking at nothing. "Leave it a few days. If you're going to sneak out, you've got to time it right."

She gazed at him, horrified and admiring in equal amounts. "You are going to get out?"

"Might be the only option if things get a lot worse. Even if they get the disease under control, you've got to think about the infrastructure long term."

Naomi gazed across at the piles of canned food in her flat. For a moment she had an almost uncontrollable desire to ask to go with him. She pushed it down. She'd look after herself.

"So you think we'll make it to fight another day."

He smiled wryly. "Just as long as you don't go into hedgehog mode next time you bump into someone infected. I can't always promise I'll be there with a cricket bat."

High on Skye – the Ultimate Islander's blog

Fàilte! Or welcome. Välkommen i Skottland. Or whatever the fuck you want to say. I am the sometimes unemployed twenty something Skye resident. Raised in Portree, working when the tourists come in. Sitting on my arse through the winter. This is my life.

02 May 20--

Haven't checked the news online today. Post the national lockdown and there is nothing to report over on Skye other than my massive hangover. This is all something and nothing.

From: teresathekoala@noworries.net.com.au
Sent: 03 May 20-- 07:15:09
To: naomiarcher@aceserver.co.uk

Subject: Naomi, where are you?!!!

Naomi, I just sent you two emails yesterday and the second one's been returned. It says aceserver.co.uk is unknown. What the????

From: mailclient@noworriesnet.com.au
Sent: 03 May 20-- 08:02:19
To: teresathekoala@noworriesnet.com.au

Subject: Undeliverable mail

Your message entitled < Subject: Naomi, where are you ?!!!> has been returned undelivered.

Unknown domain: aceserver.co.uk

PART FOUR
Outbreak

Carnage in Sheffield: Is this the end of the world?

An information leaflet issued by the UK government yesterday warns of "violent outbursts" and "delirium" from members of the public infected with the HEMO10 virus. Eyewitnesses in Sheffield reported psychopathic violence and cannibalism more fitting for video nasties.

Steven Marsh, a 43-year-old electrician, currently house bound as the rest of the nation, was disturbed yesterday afternoon by the sound of screaming. Marsh, who lives in a fourth floor flat in a housing area, rushed to the window to see what was happening.

"There were two old women on the footpath down between our block and the next one," Marsh said. He was not sure why they were walking outside, as all residents of Sheffield have been kept house bound by the army for the last two days. He commented that he did see a dog running around the scene yapping.

There were two men attacking the old age pensioners when Marsh looked out of the window. "It was like something out of a horror film," Marsh added. "I had to get the wife to take the kids into the bedroom so they wouldn't see it."

Marsh, and other residents in the Sheffield housing area, watched helplessly as the two men – described by various eye witnesses as "blood-splattered"; "growling" and "deranged" – attacked the women, biting and tearing at flesh. The army was contacted, but no one went outside to help the old women.

"They were like wild animals," Marsh explained. "Like when you see lions killing and eating on the telly. They were eating the women. One of them had his face in the old woman's stomach."

The army arrived promptly, but it was too late. Both women were dead at this point, and there were reports of some limbs having already been dismembered from the elderly women. One of the men was eating from the abdomen of one of the victims. The two men did not appear to be able to speak or understand the orders the army were shouting to them. When they failed to move away from the bodies, they were both shot dead with a bullet to the head. The four bodies were removed from the site and the area was thoroughly cleaned and disinfected during the night.

One local human-rights supporter, not affiliated with any major organisation, has already condemned the army's response, stating that it was execution without trial. "The soldiers are not fully-trained doctors," Marianne Jackson, 19-year-old college student protested, "and they did not know for certain that the men were infected. Even if they were infected, they should not have been executed, but rather taken away for medical treatment, as per their human rights. Because of the disease, they were not aware of what they were doing, and if this had ever got to trial, no one could have convicted them for murder. The army should have been able to capture them, and a head shot was completely out of order. I for one am disgusted by the way our country is dealing with this pandemic."

When informed of the local complaint, Marsh asked: "Have you ever seen a zombie horror film? Of course they were f*****g infected."

This incident is just one in hundreds of reports of particular violent attacks by infected people. The guidelines and information issued by the government do not appear to give a realistic impression of the severity of what form a "violent outburst" will actually take; and many civilians have complained that the information leaflet makes a mockery of what is actually happening on street level.

Eyewitnesses have described behaviour of violence and pyschopathy; with infected people showing signs of extreme hunger – so desperate for food in fact that they will put their hands on, and their teeth into what ever they can find.

There have also been increased rumours and reports of army brutality. Whilst many eyewitnesses angrily disagreed with Marianne Jackson's comments; calling them "naïve" and "plain idiotic", there is a growing fear that the infected are being exterminated rather than treated at the specialist hospitals set up by the government. Unless medical staff or infected, no one is allowed access to these sites. Due to the disease's apparent effects on the human brain, when the symptoms are in full swing, the infected are to all intents and purposes unaware of what is happening to them. However, the sickness is particularly distressing for relatives, and anyone who believes they may have recently been infected.

Without any vaccination, or any known cure or treatment that the government is prepared to discuss, the question remains as to what else can be done with people who show behaviour patterns of homicidal tendency and deranged cannibalism; and for whom – rumours mount – have a hundred percent mortality rate.

Donna Sheppard - Sheffield
03 May 20--

"So this is what they're all saying on the grapevine."

Richard looked groggily up from the kitchen table. Ed was leaning at him from the other side, a little wobbly, his hair sticking up wildly. Eyes mildly puffy. The smell of whisky even from this distance. An all-nighter. Ed wouldn't admit it, but he'd probably been as worried as they had, if not more.

Midday after the longest night, and it was agreed that by even the most cautious of standards, they most definitely were not infected. On this occasion they had been spared. Greater care would be necessary in the future – you couldn't bank on luck all the time with this kind of contagion.

Ed twisted in his chair to see Naomi stood at the oven stirring canned soup. The sun came in through the kitchen window, lighting her up. She was staring dumbly out onto his garden as if she hadn't seen daylight for decades.

"You all right there, Naomi?"

She glanced over at Ed. The Ed who had turned up at her flat in the late morning once the army patrol had left, knocking on the door and wanting to know if they were all right. He had dragged them both across to his house, chattering of a celebratory lunch, comradeship and good times for all ahead. He'd started to make food, then wandered away from it, distracted. Showed them an article he'd been reading early that morning on the internet before he'd passed out. Naomi was too tired to be horrified at the mention of frenzied cannibalism. It was too surreal to credit as having actually happened.

And now she had been persuaded to finish warming up the soup because Ed's attention span had been reduced to that of a goldfish. "I'm fine," she told him. "Thanks again for having me over."

"Not a problem at all. After the night you've had, you deserve a treat."

She stared at the canned soup. This was what was going to constitute as a treat from now on?

"A long night stuck in with my brother, ha ha!"

Richard gave Ed a long look. "Are you on something?"

Ed stared back. "Just a bit of whisky. I'm fine."

"So what was this story you were going to tell us?"

"Grounds for divorce," Ed muttered, settling down at the table again. "The man was looking for grounds for divorce."

Naomi set the wooden spoon to rest over the top of the saucepan. She looked over at Richard. Ed really did appear to be loosing it. She mouthed the question – what? – at the elder brother. Richard grimaced and nudged Ed's arm. "You said they were all saying it on the grapevine."

Ed's head snapped up. "So there's this guy living over at the Poppletons. Married a real looker, but it turns out she's a right cow. He wants shot, but he needs his grounds for divorce. Wants to get it done cleanly and cheaply. Quick break.

"This happened yesterday. Sunny day. Wife was out in the garden on the sun lounger. Topping up the tan."

Something worth while worrying about these days, Naomi thought sarcastically.

"Husband walks out the house with a shot gun and blows off her face."

Naomi looked horrified. Richard coughed on surprise. This wasn't quite the story he had been expecting from Ed. "What are you talking about?"

"Grounds for divorce. He says she was infected. Getting violent. He didn't feel safe, and he'd read on the Internet that there isn't any cure. Thought the kindest thing to do would be to blow her brains out."

"Shit, you can't be serious?" Richard laughed without humour. "This sounds like an urban legend."

Urban legends for a disease that wasn't even a month old. Surely that was too quick for modern folklore. Naomi stared into the pan and thought of Ross and his unhappy marriage. Extreme circumstances could push people into doing things they wouldn't normally do. Looking for desperate measures to get out of resented arrangements and repetitive drudgery. Life is short. Life is beautiful. I want it all and I may not have long to live. Etc. etc.

Ed was shaking his head. "Straight up. The army was over quick. Took him away in a truck. Gathered up the wife's body and took her away as well. No one's heard any more of him. But they reckon they're testing her body to see if she was actually infected. Evidence to prove it was just cold bloodied murder. They've got him locked up in a cell somewhere."

"How would you know if no one's heard any more of him?" Naomi asked. Ed ignored her question.

Richard shrugged. "I suppose it's possible. People think they'll get away with murder because everyone's more worried about containing this disease. We don't have time for police investigations and trials."

"We aren't turning into savages," Naomi started.

"Aren't we? There are riots all over the world. Looting's up. Burglary, rape – and that's just from the uninfected. The army and the police have got enough to do trying to stop people from travelling; trying to stop the spread of infection."

But surely they were civilised still? They weren't animals. She thought of that man by the river; the one she had hit over the head with a stick. An online article about attacks in Sheffield. He probably would have torn her to shreds if she hadn't defended herself. And the couple on the other side of the river, regarding her as if she had been dangerous. Loaded up with rucksacks and camping gear. They were disappearing into the countryside. "You really need to be away from people."

Ed raised his eyebrows. "Probably so. Richard's wishing he'd never come to visit."

"It's easy to know what you should have done in retrospect."

"Why don't you try and get out now?" Naomi asked.

Ed looked angry at this suggestion. "He's not going without me. And I'm not going without Emma."

Richard looked mildly unimpressed by this premature devotion but made no comment. "Now's not the time.

Everyone's panicking and trying to get out. And the army's still in control and keeping everyone in town. I don't want to get caught up in all that."

"Pick your moment and sneak out the back way," Ed nodded appreciatively.

"Something like that."

"But the ring road's all blocked," Naomi said.

"Which is why this isn't something to do in haste."

"I suppose," she looked out of the kitchen window again onto Ed's sunny back garden. And then when they had gone, she wouldn't even have the company of her neighbours. Even if she could get out of York, she wouldn't have anywhere to go. Even she even had enough sense of how to get there.

High on Skye – the Ultimate Islander's blog

Fàilte! Or welcome. Välkommen i Skottland. Or whatever the fuck you want to say. I am the sometimes unemployed twenty something Skye resident. Raised in Portree, working when the tourists come in. Sitting on my arse through the winter. This is my life.

03 May 20--

More coherent today.

Caught up with the news. It looks fucking scary out there. Is this stuff for real? I can't believe we're sinking into our own international horror film. Us islands are all right though. We'll sit it out with our whisky and when all the diseased have died off, we'll move on with our lives.

Some people are worried here. The other night I was at a party. My friend's girlfriend said she was frightened about this disease – what ever they're calling it these days – and she made a special trip to Uig. Uig! What? To go to the Fairy Glen to leave an offering for the fairies. As if that's going to save her. It's unbelievable what people will turn to when they're really frightened. I am glad to say the rest of Scotland is being strong about this. Scotland the brave. Oh yeah.

COMMENT: Eloise – Paris, France
You are a monster! What comments you write. Do you understand people are dying? You sit and wait for us to die off? This is a human tragedy. I saw my grandmother killed in the street yesterday. It disgusts me how the islands are closing up and ignoring the world. You disgust me.

Naomi returned to her own flat later in the afternoon. Alone. Now that it was obvious neither she nor Richard had been infected, the alarm was switched off, and neither needed to be watched. Of course Richard and Ed would stay in Ed's house. Of course she would be alone.

She sat by the living room window and slowly made arrows. She didn't even know why, because presumably it would be a long time before the archery club would be meeting up for a social again. So much for all those worries about the AGM.

She had a CD playing in the background. Calming music. Everything is ok. She saw Ed on the first floor of his house. He glanced out of the window, half heartedly waved at her. Naomi raised her hand but he had already stepped out of view.

The army patrol drove by. Nothing to see or report.

At five o'clock there was a sudden drop in electricity. The ceiling light – which she had to have on so early on account of the flat being generally dark – dimmed and the CD abruptly stopped. A second then the electricity surged again, the bulb glowing full force. Naomi continued to stare at the ceiling, thinking that this was the beginning. A portent. The infrastructure would eventually crumble if everything remained in lockdown.

Putting aside the arrows, she walked across to the back of the living room and opened the kitchenette doors. Made some toast and a cup of tea, then flopped onto the settee. A collection of paperback books were gathering like drifting leaves. Aside from the terror of the virus, this ban on travel, this nervous hiding that would eventually lead to apathy; there was very little to do apart from read and reflect upon life. Company would have been nice; or perhaps it would have been a curse. Locked in with the same people twenty-four hours a day. Never able to get out and see someone different.

Her Internet connection was still down, so she couldn't send emails or check the news online. She turned on the television – two of the channels already weren't working. The others were only showing pre recorded programmes and news bulletins on a regular basis.

She started to read a book she had read years ago; couldn't really remember the plot. It wasn't gripping, although she could remember being enthralled by it at one time. Lying down on the settee, she read on as her eyes sagged. Her head on a cushion. She fell asleep.

It was dark when she woke up with a jolt. A movement like convulsions up her throat. Something was wrong. She remained half burrowed in the settee, glancing nervously through the shadows of her flat. There is was again – a thump and then a shout. Angry shouts; strange noises. So close and yet muffled as if she was underwater.

Someone screamed.

Naomi clutched the cushion to her chest and squeezed her eyes shut – as if that would make it all go away.

A faded shout. It sounded like 'what are you doing?' A furious question, more frightened than angry now. Her body crunched as Naomi realised the noise was coming from downstairs – her neighbours below were fighting again. This happened now and then, which was hardly surprising considering there were two grown adults living together in a one-bedroom flat as claustrophobically small as her own. But there was something different to this domestic situation.

The front door slammed open and running footsteps were heard. Naomi sat up. This wasn't happening in her flat. She was safe. Gingerly creeping across the carpet, she knelt at the single living room window, resting her arms on packets of mashed potato powder to look out onto the street.

It was night outside. The woman was stood on the far side of the road under a street light. Her clothes were dishevelled and her left forearm appeared to be bleeding. She clutched at it as a dying infant. There was betrayal on her face. She looked back at the building. "You've been infected, haven't you?"

There was no reply as such, only a muddle of growls and guttural sounds. Naomi leant forward slightly to see the top of the man's head as he staggered from the front door. Oh Christ, there was infection right below her. Last night she and Richard had sat up worrying they were about to die, and all the time it had been festering downstairs. Mere metres away from her.

She had locked the door, hadn't she? She watched as the man ran towards the woman. Naomi thought back through her day, returning to her own home. She had locked the door. Besides, it was a yale lock. It was always automatically locked. She didn't dare go downstairs to check. Didn't want to make a sound. No attention to the fact that she was close by. What if he tried to break in to get at her?

Someone must have rung the army number. Although surely this was too quick a response? The sound of a motor engine distracted the man from pursuing the woman. An army jeep appeared, shuddering to an abrupt halt; the soldiers inside shaken with the effect. One of them lifted a rifle and aimed at the man. There was an awful moment – no one moving or speaking – then the sound of the shot and the infected man dropped to the floor, a feather protruding from his neck.

The woman started screaming: "You've killed him!"

"It's a tranquiliser dart!" the jeep shouted back at her. "Stay where you are. Medical attention is on its way."

She sank to the pavement, whimpering in street light.

"Madam," one of the soldiers called over to her. Naomi noted that no one made any attempt to get out of the jeep. "Have you been bitten?"

She continued to cry.

"We can see you are bleeding."

The woman looked at her arm. The reality occurring to her. "Oh god," she wailed. "Does this mean I'm going to die?"

The soldiers hesitated longer in their reply than they should have. "The ambulance is on its way. Don't worry. You're going to get help."

A few very long minutes later, an ambulance pulled up beside the jeep. No sirens or flashing lights. It wasn't necessary anymore. No one was travelling; the message getting through that they weren't to be allowed out of the city. Most had given up trying to escape and resigned themselves behind locked doors. Streets were relatively empty. The passenger door to the ambulance opened and a man in a white coat tentatively looked out. Two of the soldiers stood up and aimed their rifles at the infected man now sleeping in the middle of the road.

"We've got the man covered. You need to tend to the woman. She's been bitten."

Carrying a small case that looked like a toolbox, the man slipped out of the ambulance and hurried over to the crying woman. He knelt down beside her and patted her shoulder as if that would make everything all right. "Don't worry," he told her. "We're going to take care of you." He took a roll of bandage out of the box and proceeded to wrap it around the woman's arm.

Whilst this was happening, a black van came onto the street and pulled up on the pavement. The engine was switched off but no one got out of the van. The soldiers were fully aware it had arrived, but made no visible reaction to it. Naomi leaned forward, forgetful of herself as she was caught up in the awful drama. What was happening? Is this the response she and Richard would have received if they had been good little citizens and rung the army post, concerned that they might be infected?

The man in the white coat led the woman to the ambulance. The engine was still running. The pair got in the back of the vehicle and shut the door. The ambulance drove away down the road.

One of the soldiers got down from the jeep.

A door below opened as her next door neighbour from the first floor stuck his head out. "Are we going to be evacuated now?"

"Evacuated?" The solider looked at him as if he were an idiot.

"This is the second time this has happened here."

Naomi clutched at the packets in front of her; terrified a nosey neighbour was about to reveal what had happened to her and Richard.

"And where would we evacuate you to?"

"Somewhere where there isn't any infection."

The solider shook his head, pitying another fool who hadn't bothered to think what the world had actually become. "Sir, get back in your house and lock your doors and windows. Until further notice, all citizens are to stay in their homes and under no circumstances leave."

"But I'm running out of food."

"There'll be food supplies delivered the day after tomorrow."

"But…"

The soldier shifted the grip on his rifle slightly. "Get back in your house."

The door slammed shut.

The sliding door on the side of the black van was opened and a figure in a white decontamination suit, the hood pulled up, stepped out. A face mask with breathing apparatus was pushed up onto the top of his head like an alternative sun hat. The latest fashion of necessity. He had a small kit bag in one hand.

"Why wasn't that man dressed in full protective gear?" he barked angrily at the soldiers.

"What man?"

"The doctor."

One of the men still in the jeep; possibly the man in charge, looked irritated by the question. "Does no one keep you up to date with what's going on?"

"What, have they realised that infection is just a myth?" The man in the suit was distinctly sarcastic. It didn't sound as though he had had much sleep.

"That man wasn't a doctor. He was just a porter at the hospital. He was bitten half an hour ago and he's agreed to work with the ambulance pick up service for a couple of hours."

"You're sending infected people out to work?"

"They're all right for the first couple of hours. People are terrified," the commander almost screamed at the man on the pavement. "We're having a really hard time trying to persuade them to go away in the ambulance with a guy dressed up like he's away to the fucking moon. Now get on with your job and clear this mess up."

The man muttered something too low for Naomi to hear.

He pulled his breathing apparatus down over his face as a second figure got of the van. It was a woman this time. "What's the condition of the man?"

"We shot him with a tranquiliser."

She nodded and observed from a distance as her colleague, somewhat nonchalantly, walked up to the casualty and rolled him over. He pulled back one of the eyes to check, rolled up the man's sleeve and examined the underarm. Opened the mouth and looked inside with a torch. He stood up and took a few steps away. "This one's really far gone."

A third figure came out of the van carrying a large roll of something. The first man opened his kit bag on the ground, looking for something. The third figure stood at the feet of the infected man. The first took a pistol out of the bag, walked up to the sleeping figure and shot him between the eyes.

Naomi ducked down below the window. The gun had obviously been fitted with a silencer, but she had still heard that whistle and a thud. The man was now dead.

The commander stood up abruptly in the jeep. "What the hell are you doing?"

The woman looked at him. "Does no one keep you up to date with what's going on? There's no cure. Staff are dropping like flies trying to deal with the infected. We did that guy a favour."

The third figure unrolled a thick black body bag. The two of them got the body zipped up. They carried it across to the van; bringing forth large boxes, cleaning equipment and other paraphernalia. One remained out on the street to disinfect the tarmac where blood had splattered. The others went into the house. They checked there was no one else in the flat. They emptied the flat of whatever food items were present, putting them in specially sealed boxes to be carried back to the van. They spent the next few hours decontaminating the flat.

Naomi's heart tried to force its way out of her throat when her landline started ringing. Scrabbling desperately across the floor, she picked up the phone, sweat pouring from her body. Please don't ring. Don't let them know I'm here. "Hello?" she whispered into the phone.

There was a pause. "Naomi?"

"Yes," she breathed.

"Are you all right?"

She paused. She didn't know how to answer a question like that. "Who is this?"

"It's Richard." He paused. "You know, Ed's brother. We've been watching what's going on from upstairs. Have you seen?"

She nodded.

"Downstairs from you."

"Yes," she finally breathed into the phone.

"And you're all right?"

"Yes."

"Don't worry. They've taken them away now. They'll get the place cleaned out and that'll be in the end of it."

Naomi felt her body sag. She thought about that crying woman. Her boyfriend inert on the ground. "Did you hear what they said about the man from the ambulance?"

She heard a sharp intake a breath. Perhaps he had thought of what might have happened, if they had called the army. "Yes, I heard."

"Do you think they'll kill her now or wait until she starts attacking people?"

"I don't know."

The next morning was bright and sunny. The blood splatters had been removed from the road. Back to former appearances, but it wasn't the same. Something had gone. Having seen three of their neighbours ravaged by this virus – all by varying degrees, but all with the same outcome, one presumed – people were nervous, growing in despondency. This wasn't something to read about in the newspapers; something that happened to other people. They were wondering who would be next.

Richard sat on a chair by the front window and stared silently out onto the street. There was a mug of tea on the windowsill, untouched and cold. He'd been there for an hour. Ed wasn't sure if he was standing guard or just lost in his thoughts, but either way, it was tense and not exactly reassuring. This atmosphere was stifling. When were the government going to get their finger out and get this sorted?

Ed walked into the room and coughed to announce his arrival. Richard made no sign that he had noticed.

"You get through to Naomi last night?"

"Yes," Richard replied, not bothering to look over at his brother. "She's all right."

"Did she hear much of what was going on in the flat?"

"I didn't quiz her on the details."

"No," Ed sighed, flopping down onto the settee. "Wouldn't have seemed like the right time. Did you see them carrying all those boxes out? They must have found the car keys as well. I saw one of them come out to find out which cars went with the flat. They drained the tanks of petrol. Bloody scavengers."

"I suppose they want all spare supplies for the authorities before looters come by," Richard said quietly. "Besides, it's not like those two are going to need them now."

"Well, he certainly won't."

Richard shifted in his seat to regard his brother for the first time that morning.

"And according to Mr Pessimistic, she won't either," Ed sighed.

Richard turned back to the window.

Ed took his mobile phone out of his jacket pocket and juggled it from one hand to the other. He couldn't decide what was worse: this constant feeling of impending death or the infuriating boredom of sitting around with no idea of when or how this was all to end. "Do you remember that bloke I was telling you about from the Poppletons?"

"What?"

"You know, shot his wife in the face. They executed him at dawn."

Richard scoffed. "I think you're bloody day dreaming."

"No, seriously," Ed contested. "They executed him. They tested his wife's corpse, and proved that she hadn't been infected. So he's a murderer, but no one has any time for court cases and prison sentences – he's just one more worry they could do without. They couldn't just let him go. Everything's teetering on anarchy…"

"You get that line out of a blog?" Richard asked dryly.

Ed ignored him. "So they shot him. Kills two birds with one stone. They don't need to work out what to do with him, and it sends out a message to everyone else: murder is still illegal."

"But last night it was acceptable to shot that man."

"Well, I…"

Richard turned fully away from the window. "I'm not going to dispute that. There's nothing they could have done for him, so it probably was the kindest thing they could have done. But if they had found the wife had been infected, what would they have done?"

"Well, it was still murder," Ed started uncertainly.

"But he would have been putting her out of her misery. He would have been stopping the spread of infection. They'd have probably sent him home with a shot gun."

"Jesus, you're cynical."

"It's not really the age of the idealist anymore, is it?"

Ed's mobile phone started ringing, and he was glad of the distraction. Richard could get very grim at times. Especially when it came to issues of life. It was probably shooting all those wildlife films; watching animals tear each other to shreds in a bid to survive. It was nature's way – that was probably Richard's answer to everything.

"Ed?"

"Emma!" Ed burst out, pleased to hear her voice. Finally, something positive to focus on. "Are you finally getting a day off that job of yours?"

She paused. As if Ed was an idiot sometimes. "We're not really doing days off anymore in the health service. I've just been given a few hours off to sleep. I just thought I'd ring and see if you're ok before I go to bed."

"You're not going to bed now!"

"Ed, I haven't slept for two days." She sounded near to tears.

"But you live right in the centre of town. It's not safe." As if their little road in the suburbs was. "You don't want to go back to work. That place is dangerous. You might get infected."

"I'm not working with the virus directly at the moment. I was transferred over to the maternity unit to help out."

"The maternity unit," Ed scoffed, "Now is hardly the time for having babies."

"Yeah, if only we'd had nine months' warning, we could have all quit sex for a year."

"You're not pregnant are you?"

Emma sighed heavily into the phone. She just wanted to sleep. "No, I'm not."

"Look, you want to get yourself up here. York's not safe to stay in. We're going to get up to my brother's place. He lives in a little village in the middle of nowhere."

Richard's expression dropped as if to say 'what the...?'

"But I can't get up to you."

"Seriously," Ed told her. "You have to get yourself up here. Forget about the job. We're getting out of here and I'm not going without you."

"Now wait a minute," Richard stood up.

Ed put up a hand to make it clear he wasn't going to listen to a word from his elder brother. "Leave your flat and get yourself up here now."

"But we're not supposed to leave our houses. How am I supposed to get all the way up to Huntington?"

"Well, you're a jogger."

"You're suggesting I jog all the way up Huntington road and if I see the army, what, just give them the finger?"

Ed was stuck for a moment. He didn't remember Emma being quite this argumentative. It must be the lack of sleep. She'd soon mellow out when they got to the countryside. And a nurse would be a really useful person to have. "No, of course not. Just pack the essentials in a rucksack and jog up here. Take the side streets; go up that disused railway bit. Then you could sneak up the side of the Foss."

"You mean the river?"

"Yes."

Emma thought over the proposition.

"Seriously, it's getting too dangerous here. The only way we're going to survive is out in the countryside."

"All right," she agreed, although she did not sound convinced. "I'll come up now. If you're sure it'll be all right."

"It will be. Just keep moving and don't stop for anyone. Do you want me to come down and meet you somewhere?"

"No," she started slowly. "It'll just be more conspicuous. I'll see you soon."

Ed pressed the end button and set his phone down on the sideboard. He wouldn't be able to settle until she got here. He would be relieved beyond description when she arrived at his door. Then he would be ready to leave York.

"Are you turning me into some kind of Noah's Ark?"

He had forgotten Richard was still in the room. "What are you talking about?"

"I don't even know whether I am going to try and leave town. I haven't even figured out how I'm going to cross the ring road. And you're inviting your friends?"

"Emma is not just a friend."

"I wasn't aware she was anything more than a casual acquaintance."

Ed was surprised by just how irritated Richard looked. His elder brother, he who was always so chilled out. He whose philosophy on life was that there was no point worrying about anything, because either there was a solution you could be getting on with, or there wasn't, in which case, why worry? Besides which, Richard had always been the practical one who had found ways through all kinds of awkward situations.

"Look, even if I figure out how to cross the ring road without being seen; even if I get back home, we can't be hoying half the population of York with us. We just won't be able to support ourselves."

"I don't know what you're talking about. Many hands may light work."

"I'm talking about food. You're not going to be able to nip down the shops for a pint of milk and a bag of nuts whenever you feel like it."

"We've still got food. I've got a week's worth of pizzas in the freezer. Emma won't eat much. Anyway, didn't that army lad say they were going to bring round supplies tomorrow?"

"I wouldn't hold much hope on those till you've seen them."

"Well, we'll be self sufficient. You've got a big garden at your place."

Richard sighed irritably. Ed had no comprehension of how tough things could get if the country crumbled too far. "A society that relies on its supermarket to always stock everything they might need doesn't appreciate how much time and space is needed when people have to feed themselves from scratch."

"All right, so I haven't been roughing it round the world. You want to bring some tips from Papa New Guinea to the table? Roast man flesh with mashed potato?"

"Don't be an arse, Ed." Cannibalism wasn't Papa New Guinea's thing, certainly not these days, anyway, Richard thought grimly – it was a survival instinct for the infected. "I'm going to have to get out for a bit."

"But we're not allowed out."

"I'm just going across the road," Richard told him, stalking out of the front door.

Ed locked the door after him and watched through the glass panelling as Richard crossed the deserted road and went up to Naomi's front door. He glanced at his watch. A couple of minutes at best had passed since he had spoken to Emma. This was going to be the longest half hour of his life.

It was whilst Naomi and Richard were giggling over the longbow that Ed started hammering on the front door.

The morning had become more dreamlike than her subconscious could have created on its best attempt. Richard had come over to visit – as if social calls were completely normal in a country under martial law and diseased with a virulent, incurable virus. He needed a break from Ed, he mentioned illusively before looking for a distraction to interrupt Naomi from asking questions.

"You know, I've never had a go with one of these in my life."

It was more interesting than try to loose herself in the dull paperback she was persevering with (books could hardly be cast aside, for who knew if there ever would be any new books now?) and company was something she was craving more than water.

Naomi had taken her longbow out of the case and strung it up. Richard had looked mildly surprised by how casually she put pressure on; not worried that it might snap. Once strung, she offered it to Richard.

"It's light," he commented, moving to pull back the string with a couple of fingers as if it required no more strength than unravelling a ball of wool. His eyes widened slightly. "You shoot with this thing?"

"Yes. I know the poundage is quite high, but you're trying to pull it back in the wrong way, anyway."

"You must build up quite a bit of strength in your shoulders with a hobby like this."

She shrugged. "It's a gradual thing. And my bows are relatively very light compared to some of the guys who go to archery club." Go to archery club. As if it were still a going concern.

Ed started to hammer his fists on Naomi's front door. They didn't realise it was Ed. Naomi looked at Richard. Now what? Her neighbours below had been taken away in the night. One of the other flats on the ground floor was vacant possession. Who would call?

"Richard!"

"It's Ed," Richard muttered, gritting his teeth. He had been hoping to get a longer break from his brother.

"It's been half an hour now," Ed explained as Richard let him into the flat. The door was locked up again, the two brothers coming up the stairs. "She said she was going to run. She should be here by now."

"What are you talking about?"

Ed paused, his worry halted as he took in Naomi's flat. She really was odd. There were stacks of food – cans and packets – as if she'd recently looted the nearby supermarket. And there she was in the middle of it all, like Robin Hood, a long bow taller than herself in one hand. "You two off to catch dinner?"

"We were just looking at it."

Richard wasn't going to get side tracked into Ed taking the piss. "What about Emma? Have you not tried ringing her mobile?"

"She's not picking up."

Emma? She had heard the name before. Naomi thought back, and remembered the slim woman with blonde curls at the salsa night. "She's coming over here?" She looked horrified, thinking of her own stroll in the local countryside. People really shouldn't leave their homes. "You didn't tell her to walk through York to get here?"

Ed scowled. "She's jogging."

Naomi walked up to the window. It did look deceptively peaceful out there. Like a sun-drenched walk by the river. Away from roads and houses. Supposedly far away from people. She wondered if the army would have picked up that man yet. Perhaps he had got up himself and crossed the little footbridge over to Earswick. Or maybe he had died in the grass, his festering corpse now rotting into the field.

There was a strangled cry outside. A small figure appeared down the road, dressed in a blue vest top and jogging trousers;

a rucksack strapped on her back. She was crying, gasping and struggling as she jogged forward. There was something dark on her neck. Blood trickled down, stained in her clothes. A few metres behind, another woman followed. This second woman was covered in blood, and yet she seemed more energised and steady in herself as she jogged. Animal sounds followed. Her teeth showed.

Naomi felt sick. "There's someone in the road."

The two men joined her at the front of the living room. Ed's hands slammed up against the glass. He opened the window, flinging it wide open, shouting Emma's name. Emma made a whimpering response, but was in too much of a panic to look for the source of the call.

"Have to kill it," Ed was talking to himself, looking at his surroundings desperately for something to lob out of the window. He reached for a large can of soup, then saw a line of arrows Naomi finished making last night and picked one up. Snatching the bow off Naomi, he made a pose as they did in the films and made to shoot the arrow but only managed to draw back the string a few centimetres before the bow stopped like a stubborn donkey.

"What the?" He looked desperately at Naomi. "You have to kill her."

"Kill her?" she asked, horrified as he pushed the weapon into her hands. "What do you mean? Kill Emma?"

"No! Kill the monster!"

"But that's a person. That's murder..."

"Kill it!" Ed screamed in her face.

Emma was almost upon their section of the road. Naomi's chest tightened. She didn't dare breath. If only someone could put it all on pause and give her chance to think. It was no distance at all for her to shoot, but she had never taken down a living target, and she didn't think she could do it now.

Ed turned to run down the stairs.

"It's not murder. This isn't human," Richard spoke.

"Of course that's human."

"And where are you going to draw the line? That woman is already infected. She's already dead," Richard said. Down the stairs they could hear Ed swearing and struggling with the lock. "When he gets out there, he's not going to think to lock the door after him. She might come up here next and attack us."

Naomi picked up an arrow and set it to the bow. She drew back the string across her body and aimed out of the window. She was terrified and she wasn't even in danger, up on the first floor, out of reach from this horror as if she were only watching it on the television. She felt her eyes brimming up with tears. She wasn't cut out for this kind of survival.

"Aim for the path she's going to run into."

Naomi let go of the bowstring. There was a dull thud, a small, insignificant spray of red. The bloodied female figure dropped to the ground. Richard left her side. In the road, Emma was still running, hysterical, stumbling in circles. Unaware that she was safe. Safe for a couple of hours at least. Ed was trying to grab her, pull her in and get her off the street. People would watch from their windows but they would have enough sense now not to go outside.

Richard appeared on the street. He ran across to the figure lying on her back. The arrow had gone through her right eye and into her brain. Killed instantaneously. What kind of an aim was that? Pure shot out of Hastings. He looked up at the window where Naomi was still placed; a faded image watching on. Looking back at the body, the bloodied teeth, the tears on her arms, stains on her clothes. Her belly looked a little swollen. No time to think. He grasped the shaft of the metal arrow and pulled it from her skull.

Naomi dropped her bow. She turned from the window and ran downstairs. Through the blazing opening, sunlit and bright, she could see Ed as he caught hold of Emma's arm and pulled her sobbing frame to him. Richard stood back as he got the arrow out of the woman's head. Ed didn't notice her, but Richard did. He began to raise his hand as if to tell her not to come out. As if she would have. Naomi slammed the door shut and started to turn all the locks.

When he had gone back into the house, Emma had been screaming. She looked as though she was about to explode from sound, pressure or the immense terror pressing down. Her face was bright red from the exhaustion; tears were streaming down her skin. Her voice was ragged and yet she continued; shaking hands flapping around her.

There was no point in pretending. She didn't even have enough time left to go through the emotional process of knowing she had contracted an illness and was going to die. She couldn't cover over the marks and pretend it was nothing. Convince herself and everyone else that there was nothing to worry about.

She had been bitten. A little blood went a long way, and although there were drying rivers on her clothes, the wound was only really superficial. Superficial but more than enough. If you looked closely enough you could see the teeth marks in her skin.

Richard locked the door and stood at the side of the room. Who knew how this one was going to play out.

"Oh god, you're going to call them, aren't you?" she gasped, genuinely frightened as she looked from one uninfected brother to the other.

"Them? What are you…?"

"The army!" Emma interrupted Ed. "You're supposed to call the army when someone gets infected. They come and pick you up and take you away. And there's so many now and they don't know what to do with them and they say they're just killing them…"

"What?"

Emma wiped her eyes with the back of a blood-stained hand. The tears kept coming.

"Is that's what happening with infected people?" Richard sounded distinctly calm in the mist of their panic.

Emma glanced over at him; her gulping sobs subsiding a little. "It's not official, but everyone's saying it."

"Everyone at the hospital?"

She nodded.

"No one's going to call the army." Ed decided, gripping her by the wrists to stop her hands trembling. "I am going to look after you."

She stared up at him, thinking he was mad. "That woman bit me."

"I know."

"But you don't understand. I've seen what happens to people."

"So have we. There's been a few performances out on our street. But that doesn't have to be you." His hands squeezed tighter around her wrists. "There's a girl across the road who knows a guy working on the cure."

"There's a cure? I haven't heard about this."

"It's not official yet…"

"But I'd have heard."

"No you wouldn't," Ed said sharply. "Naomi's friend works right at the top. There's a cure coming. I'm going to keep you safe until the cure's ready. Now, do you feel better?"

Richard watched in horrified wonder. Emma nodded meekly. Who knew whether she really believed Ed or not. She had stopped crying at least.

"Do you want to go upstairs and get a shower? I'll see if I have something you can borrow to wear."

"All right," she said quietly.

Across the road, Naomi was sitting in an empty bath in a locked bathroom. She was feeling cold and had pulled on her winter coat before retreating to what she considered the most secure room in her flat. Hunched forward, her mobile phone in both hands, she flicked through the contacts list till she reached Rudi's number. Pressed dial and listened to the ringing tone.

"Hello?"

She felt an overwhelming sense of relief to hear Rudi's voice. A point of normality from her life was still alive.

"Hello, Naomi, are you all right?" He sounded as though he was starting to panic.

She smiled wearily. "I'm fine. I was ringing to hear how things are."

He paused, not believing her. "I'm working hard."

"Found a cure yet?"

Rudi made a disgruntled noise. "We're a long, long way off that."

"I just found myself worrying because you're working so close with this disease. That you might get infected."

"We are taking full bio safety precautions." He sounded bored by it all. "There is nothing to worry about at my end. They are so unbelievably careful with us. They daren't do anything else. They need us to solve this."

"You'll do it."

"We'll see."

Naomi coughed suddenly, and felt moisture spring to her eyes. "I shot someone today," she whispered into the phone.

"What? Did you just say what I think you said? Do you mean an infected person? I didn't think York was that badly infected. Not compared to other places."

Naomi closed her eyes. If this wasn't "that bad", she didn't want to think about what other cities were going through. "She was infected. She was chasing this woman. I think she'd bitten her. It looked as though she was going to kill her."

"Did you read that web link I sent you?"

"Yes."

"Then you know you did the right thing," Rudi told her, almost scolded her. "That woman was already dead. As good as. It's the best way to stop the spread of infection." He paused, an uncertain silence. "No one's attacked you; I mean, no one's...."

"I'm not infected," she told him. "No one's bitten me."

"You're staying in your flat, right?"

She didn't dare tell him that she'd been stupid enough to take a morning stroll by the river a few days ago. What felt like a lifetime ago. Back when everything seemed normal, and every day activities such as walking in the fresh air were certainly not a matter for concern.

"I'm hiding away in my flat."

"Best thing to do for now. Try to ride it out. I just wish you were somewhere a little more remote."

"Remote?"

"In the countryside."

"But I'll be all right here?"

"I'm sure you'll be fine. This thing will burn itself out if everyone stays in their homes. But our infrastructure is collapsing. Once the threat of infection is over, we've got a lot of rebuilding to do, and life in the countryside might be more sustainable."

"So you're sure this will be over soon?"

She needed positive and definite answers. He didn't feel he could give anything. Six months ago he wouldn't have thought a virus this virulent and this widespread could have brought the world to its knees just as quickly as it had done. There didn't seem to be any guarantees left.

"It's not the end of the world," he eventually said, not feeling that convinced in himself. "There will be survivors and you will be one of them. Just look after yourself."

She was crying properly now. No one believed it was going to be that simple. "Okay."

"Look, I've got to get back in the lab. I'll speak to you soon."

Even that felt like a promise no one could be sure they'd be able to keep.

From: Naomikiwi@noworriesnet.com.au
Sent 04 May 20-- 07:02:13
To: teresathekoalo@noworriesnet.com.au

Subject: I am ok – today is the 4 May.

Teresa,

The UK servers went down. The infrastructure is going down point blank. What do you mean it's just media hysteria? Are you mental? I have your email saved on my laptop and I can't believe you wrote that. We are living our worst nightmares here.

I had to set up an account with an Australian email service. We have to connect to the Internet through Richard's mobile now. At least we still have that.

This isn't just some little virus that will go away. Did you hear what happened in Ireland? Of course we've got it in York. It makes people turn bloody psychotic. Two days ago I was attacked outside my flat. I was terrified I'd got it. They say incubation is between 5 and 10 hours. I can't tell you how glad I am that it is two days on and I haven't turned into one of them. Now we're waiting to find out if Ed's girlfriend has it. If you suspect you're infected, you're supposed to go directly to the nearest army post. But having heard what happened in Ireland and rumours of what they're doing here... they say they're executing people. Everyone is too frightened to hand themselves in.

It's total lock down. You're not allowed to leave the town you live in. Really, you're not supposed to leave your house. There are army patrols that go by. But I don't know how they're going to enforce this. Think of all the little towns and villages. I really wish I was living out in the middle of the countryside. It's terrifying here. Like slow death.

I've never been so frightened. Naomi.

From: teresathekoala@noworriesnet.com.au
Sent: 04 May 20-- 10:02:01
To: naomikiwi@noworries.com.au

Subject: Re: I am ok – today is the 4 May.

OMG Naomi, I am so glad to hear from you. I haven't had an email from my brother for days. I keep getting this bounce back from his email. And he is not answering his phone. I am so worried.

I am sorry if I sounded as though I wasn't taking it seriously. We are getting a lot of news here, especially online. I think the government is being open to scare us into realising how lucky we are. It looks like something out of a horror film.

And you were attacked? But you're definitely ok. How is this other woman? Who is Ed? And who is Richard? I don't remember you telling me about them before.

Teresa

High on Skye – the Ultimate Islander's blog

Fàilte! Or welcome. Välkommen I Skottland. Or whatever the fuck you want to say. I am the sometimes unemployed twenty something Skye resident. Raised in Portree, working when the tourists come in. Sitting on my arse through the winter. This is my life.

04 May 20--

Just came online and saw I am being accused of being a monster. French girl, I don't even know why you're looking at my blog, but fuck off, all right? You'd be exactly the same if you were in my shoes. You forget we just see this stuff on the Internet when it's working. This isn't happening here. This is not affecting us. All we've got to do is sit around and slap the midges. Anyway, if it's so awful in Paris, surely you've got better things to do than insult me online.

PART FIVE
Slow Death

Is it time to start using the Z-word?

Let's start exactly as we mean to go on. Let's be honest.

Zombie is a word usually connected to horror films (many of the sub-standard variety) and fantasy in popular imagination. It's not a word anyone is comfortable using to describe real, cold-light-of-day life; especially these days. I asked around. "Besides which," I was told by one colleague, "Zombies are dead. These people are just infected with a disease."

Such a casual attitude is undoubtedly shared by others who have yet to come face to face with the effects of the HEMO10 virus. Even the earlier comment that zombies are dead shows a misunderstanding of the old culture of zombies, and also what has broken out across the globe. Truth be told, zombies might actually be closer to the reality than we'd like to admit.

Tales of zombies: the dead rising from their graves, shuffling around after people and groaning, but not a lot more; originating from the Caribbean and the culture of Voodoo. All folktales have their origins in reality; more often than not leading to wildly misinterpretations of the facts. In the case of zombie folklore, bodies were dug up out of graves, apparently coming back to life, groaning and shuffling and generally mentally inert. The misunderstanding that fed the myth revolves around the point that these people were never dead in the first place.

Voodoo practitioners would give the zombie-to-be poison taken from the pufferfish to send them into a deep sleep – essentially appearing physically dead to the outside world. The person would be buried. Underground they were still alive. When the coffin was dug up, the poison having worn off, the person would appear to come to life again. The notion of the living dead – this shuffling and groaning – is not because the person was part dead, but was actually due to brain damage. Not from the poison, but from the lack of oxygen in the coffin underground.

And just as the real-life zombies of the Caribbean were not technically the living dead, neither are the victims of the HEMO10 virus, however much they resemble the artistic nightmare visions of recent films. After symptoms start to show, death usually occurs two to three days later; however, those that are kept well fed and watered have been known to survive for up to 10 days – to put this into more graphic terms, those that eat red raw meat live longest.

There have been countless reports of frenzied cannibalistic behaviour, and it is just this raw meat and blood that is necessary to keep the diseased body alive. HEMO10 is a viral hemorrhagic fever, as are its weaker cousins such as the Ebola virus and the Borna Virus. HEMO10 has a much shorter incubation period than any of these diseases, and takes a more intense and violent hold on the human body (the virus has not yet jumped the species gap) – affecting not only the body but also the mind. It also has a much higher mortality rate, currently sitting at one hundred percent.

Viral hemorrhagic fevers are a group of diseases characterised by fever and bleeding. In the past diseases such as the Ebola virus have been frightening enough, with a high mortality rate and warranting the highest bio safety in health and research circles, at level four. The sudden appearance and international outbreak of HEMO10 has pushed any fear about nasty diseases as Ebola far out of mind, and brought forth the reality of 'zombie' invasions that used to be seen only in popular entertainment.

There is no cure and there is no vaccine. Some scientists have commented that our best hope of survival is to sit this one out. The positives with this disease are: 1. It's not airborne (and I have been assured by various people of medical and scientific backgrounds that we are well and truly screwed if it ever mutates into an airborne variant); and 2. The disease progresses so quickly in the human body that it's going to kill itself off. A fortnight after first infection, any victim will be dead. If we can get through so many weeks without any new infections, then we will be able to start the task of rebuilding our countries, confident we are now disease-free. Some diseases don't manage long-term planning and effectively commit biological suicide in the end. A potential example may be the mysterious sweating sickness that ravaged Tudor England in the 1500s, disappearing as abruptly as it appeared. At the date of writing this article, neither of these points bring much cheer.

Looking to the future in the most positive light, we will have a massive rebuild on our hands. With chaos nearing anarchy, it is impossible at this stage to predict just how severe the population drop will be. Even when infection is no longer an immediate threat, there will be pressing issues such as provision of food and clean water, as well as rebuilding medical services for all the other ailments in the health rainbow that will continue to crop up as we try to get on with life. With infrastructure and society crumbling as it is now, when this nightmare does finally end, the survivors will be faced with an immense challenge and a very different world to live in. The Z-word doesn't even begin to encapsulate what we've got ahead of us.

Martin Sandberg
London, May 20—

Ed felt physically sick. Yet he couldn't admit to it. He didn't want to, and had to force up the smile. Convince everyone that this was going to be all right. He was going to have to go over the road and speak to Naomi soon. He'd ask Richard – who was currently across the road – to question her, but Ed felt he needed to hear the answers first hand. Richard had a habit of sticking his own interpretation on to everything.

After showering and swapping her vest top for one of Ed's T-shirts, Emma had gone for a lie down, complaining of feeling weary. She had curled up in Ed's bed and fallen asleep. Ed didn't know if he would have been able to sleep with the possibility of infection so apparent.

She had slept through most of the afternoon, and when she came down the staircase and into the living room, it was obvious that she hadn't escaped.

There was red blotching on her skin around her neck – all that was visible outside of the T-shirt. What might have been taken as an excess of crying was definitely a reddening of the eyes. Hadn't they mentioned some kind of eye-bleeding in that information sheet they'd dropped off? Ed hadn't paid it much attention as he now wished he had done so.

Emma leaned against the door frame, holding her stomach and groaning a little.

"How are you feeling?"

"Woozy." She looked over at him. She was frightened. "Quite weak."

"Are you hungry?"

"Ravenous."

Ed stepped backwards. It was an unconscious reaction, but as soon as his body started to shift, they were both aware of it. What it meant. He felt terrible. She needed his support now, not his revulsion. It was bad enough that she was infected; she didn't want to see the people who cared for her pushing her away. Besides, she was hardly a slathering monster. Perhaps she would only suffer mild symptoms.

"I'll get something out of the freezer," he said, perhaps a little too brightly. Hurrying off to the kitchen. Looking for tasks to keep hands busy and minds distracted.

Emma followed him to the kitchen doorway. "I feel so weak," she said. "Like a bad cold."

"Well, let's get something cooked to warm you up. You fancy pizza? I've got margarita, meat feast..."

"Meat feast."

"Okay." Ed took the frozen pizza out and tossed it onto the kitchen worktop. Emma watched as he switched on the oven.

"Where's your...?" she closed her eyes, putting her fingers to her forehead.

"Where's my what?"

She opened her eyes and gazed up at him. She looked drunk. Glazed. "Brother." She made it sound as though it were an effort to force the word out.

"Oh, Richard? He's over at Naomi's at the moment," Ed answered off-handed. "She lives across the road. Actually, she's the one who shot that woman."

"Woman."

"You know, who was chasing you." Ed winced. He probably shouldn't have brought up the subject. They were busy pretending everything was fine.

"She mit be."

Ed squinted at her. "What?"

"She bit me," Emma repeated as if she hadn't said anything wrong the first time.

"Yes." Ed turned to the oven. He couldn't stand to look at her. He had been certain he had been right asking her to come up here – get away from the city centre and away from the hospital. It had been the right thing to do.

Emma started coughing. Like a bad cold. She automatically put her hand up to catch the germs. When she took her hand away, she saw the blood on her fingers. She wanted to cry. She knew more than a lot of people just how awful this was going to be. And she really didn't want to die, not just yet. There was so much she wanted to do. Experiences and ambitions yet to be realised. Already she was barred from so much. Infected, she couldn't even take a simple kiss.

Ed turned around and Emma quickly wiped her hand on the side of her trousers. She smiled feebly at him. "I'm going to sit in the back garden," she told him. "It looks sunny."

Sometime during the night, Ed chained Emma up in the garden.

Richard had fallen asleep – particularly frustrating as he had purposefully stayed up waiting for his brother to go to bed. As if anyone one would be relaxed enough to slumber into unconsciousness. They had an infected woman on their property who had been bitten over ten hours ago. It was swiftly becoming less of a worry for her well-being, and more for their own health.

He had returned from Naomi's to find Emma sat on Ed's sun lounger in the back garden. She was coughing into a fist full of tissues, and when she took them away, they were surprisingly well sprayed with blood. She was taking on a sallow look, which only accentuated the red blotches creeping out from the original wound and across her skin. Her eyes were distinctly blood shot, as if vessels inside were bursting by the minute. As the evening went on she was struggling to keep a coherent sentence together. It made her increasingly angry, and at one point she even threw her cup at the back wall of the house in fury.

When Ed got up to take the plates into the kitchen, Richard followed him back into the house.

"What the hell is going on? You're enjoyed a nice summer evening meal? Have you lost the plot?"

Ed didn't answer. Stony backed; he stood and scrapped the remains of the meal into the kitchen bin.

"She needs proper care."

"She's not going anywhere."

"Something needs to be done."

Ed had slammed the plates on the kitchen worktop. "I am not calling the army. They'll just execute her. That's all they're doing now; did you know that? Of course you do. You saw what they did to that bloke out there. They don't know what else to do."

"You're going to have to do something. Bloody hell, she is deteriorating by the minute." Both men looked out of the window, for a moment wondering if she'd still be sat in the garden or running for their throats. In actual fact, she had curled up under a thick blanket on the sun lounger and appeared to be sleeping. "She's going to be uncontrollable tomorrow," Richard had pointed out. "What are you going to do then?"

Ed felt like crying. He understood that his brother was right; his practical, wise older brother was right, as always, and he didn't want to admit to it. He didn't want to accept defeat. This was Emma they were discussing; not some random figure. He had barely started this relationship, and already their hopes were finished. It wasn't fair. It just not was right. He couldn't abandon her. Not when there was still a chance.

"I'll deal with it," Ed had told him quietly.

Ed's dealing with it seemed to consist of little more than sitting out in the garden with Emma for the rest of the evening. Richard had watched from upstairs. Emma had lain still for quite a while, and later, in the dim light, had wolfed down the food Ed had brought to her. She went back to sleep, and Ed remained in the garden even when all light had gone.

Richard had intended to resolve the problem whilst his younger brother was asleep. He had fallen asleep himself, and woken in the grimy dawn; in a panic as to what had happened. He stumbled up from his chair and looked out of the window. Emma was curled up on the sun lounger, the rough blanket thrown over her.

Peering through the half open door, he noted Ed sprawled across his bed. Still time to finish this. Slipping downstairs, he went out of the front of the house and into the garage, looking for the cricket bat he had used last time.

The blood had dried into a muddy brown crust. Richard held the weight in his hands, and hesitated. This was quite different from the heat of the moment; kill or be killed. It wasn't a stranger either. He didn't really know the woman, but she had a name, a face, some kind of a relationship with his brother. It wasn't anonymous. He went back into the house.

There were lines of packets and bags on the worktop in the kitchen. All defrosting from the freezer, pools of cool water collecting around the base. Slabs of red raw meat, chicken fillets, prepared dinners. The sound of the kitchen clock was uncomfortably loud.

It was when he had one hand on the kitchen door handle that he noticed the metal peg embedded into the lawn. The heavy metal chain coiling away like a dead snake, creeping up to the sun lounger and disappearing under the blanket. He wondered for a moment if Ed had already seen sense and dealt with the inevitable himself.

As if to reply to the silent question, Emma suddenly sat up. Wide awake in the wee small hours. On the front of Ed's once-clean T-shirt there was a heavily stained beard of blood; rivulets still marked on her chin. It looked as though she had thrown up over herself. She looked over to the kitchen window and raised an arm. Tried to shout something at him, but the words came out unclearly as grunts and howls. Her mouth was a dark red hole. Her lips snarled over her teeth and she scrambled up to run at the house. She managed a couple of metres before being roughly jolted back. The chain was wrapped around her waist and criss-crossed up over her shoulders like a torture-style child harness. Richard wondered where Ed had found so much metal chain.

Richard pushed the door handle down and found it locked.

"You're not to touch her."

He turned around, cricket bat raised, to meet his crumpled brother's eye.

"I know what you're thinking, and you can forget it."

"You have to be joking."

"Drop the cricket bat."

Richard lowered his arm, but did not let go. "Have you taken a look at her this morning?" he demanded. "It's cruel to let her go on like this."

"She's going to be cured."

"Cured with what?"

"Naomi knows a guy who knows about this."

"Naomi knows a guy who knows we've got at least six months before we could even hope for a cure or a vaccine. Naomi knows a guy who knows that he doesn't understand this virus; and he knows he's the one who needs to know."

"You leave Emma alone," Ed reiterated. "I'm going to look after her."

"Ed, there's nothing you can do for her. There's only one way…"

"You so much as touch her and I will kill you."

Ed's voice was monotone. Richard didn't doubt he was being serious. Delusional from lack of sleep and misery. How could anyone think there was something that could be done? He looked out of the window. Emma was on her hands and knees, throwing up into the flower bed. Her trousers were stained and clinging; it looked as though she had soiled herself. There was a dark red patch on the sun lounger where she had been resting.

"This is my house."

Slowly, negotiating, Richard carefully stood the cricket bat on the floor, propped up against the side of a cupboard.

"I think you should keep yourself to the front of the house," Ed told him. "There's nothing back here you need concern yourself with."

Naomi was woken by the landline. She opened her eyes and glanced at the clock. It was still quite early. Why would anyone be calling her? Maybe it was bad news. Maybe? What other kind of news was there these days?

She was still wearing her clothes from yesterday. Pushing back the duvet, she wandered into the living room and picked up the phone.

"Hello?"

"Naomi?"

She squinted in the daylight. Why did the voice sound familiar?

"It's Ed."

"Ed?" she croaked. Ed had been the last person she would have expected to call. She rubbed the sleep out of her eyes, and peered out of the window in confusion. What had happened in the last twenty-four hours again? "Are you all right? How is Emma? Is she..." She didn't know how to finish that last question.

Ed took in a breath. "She's picked it up." He made it sound like a slight cold.

Naomi grimaced and slumped onto the floor, her back against the wall. The first casualty she knew. She didn't really know Emma though, to be fair; but it was the first case where she had a name, a little background history and a connection. "I'm so sorry, Ed," she said quietly. "What are you going to do?"

"I'm going to look after her."

She couldn't have heard what she thought she had. "Sorry?"

"I'm going to look after her. Look, Naomi, Richard told me you have a friend who works with diseases."

"What, Rudi?"

"I don't remember if that's the name, but does he?"

"Well, yes. He works down in London. He's working on the HEMO10 virus."

"So he'll be working on a cure."

"Eventually," she said slowly. "But they still need to fully understand the virus…"

"Of course they'll be working on a cure. The government will make them. As soon as it's ready, you get him to tell you. I'm going to look after Emma until it's ready."

Naomi squeezed her eyes shut. He obviously wasn't coping. "Ed, look…"

"Keep me up to date, all right?" Ed interrupted. "We're counting on you."

He hung up on her. He obviously didn't want to hear the truth, although deep down he already knew. What did he mean; he was going to look after her? Naomi glanced at her watch. A few more hours and it would be twenty four hours since she had been bitten. She would be a raving psychopath.

Someone knocked heavily on the door. Naomi put her hand to her mouth.

There was a second knock.

"If there's anyone in there, open up. This is the army," an impatient voice shouted from outside.

She got up and cautiously went downstairs. Leaning up to the door, she looked through the spy hole to the other side. A solider in full military gear, helmet included, was waiting outside holding a clipboard. Why was he here? Had someone reported her to the authorities – that they'd seen one of the infected chasing her; seen Richard smash the man's head to pieces with a cricket bat; seen the blood splatter over her clothes. She could see the army truck waiting in the road. Were they going to take her away? She didn't want to die. She wasn't even infected.

"I'm here about the supplies." The solider looked very bored.

Supplies. Of course, food supplies. Turning the key, she unlocked the door and pulled back the chain.

The solider gave her a sour look as she finally admitted to her presence. "Is it just yourself living here?"

"Yes."

"Name." He didn't bother to look at her anymore, pen hovering on another sheet on the clipboard.

Why did she feel as though she was in serious trouble? "Naomi," she answered quietly.

"Naomi what?"

"Ellerbeck."

"Age?"

"Thirty."

"Female," he muttered to himself, writing something down on the sheet before checking it off with some typed information at the bottom of the page. "Right, just stand still for me."

"Sorry?"

He took out a digital camera and took her photograph. "You'll be supplied with basic rations. When you've finished them, clean out the containers and keep them, or else you won't get anymore."

It sounded so final, so dire. "Are you being serious?"

He looked at her as though she were an idiot.

A young solider, probably only seventeen and just in the army, wondering what kind of a career choice this had been, left the truck with an armful of meagre, unlabeled cans and bottles. He ran up to her door and passed the items across.

Naomi took them, surprised by how light they were. "How long are these supposed to last?"

"Until we come back."

"Richard Stilton?" Another solider with a clipboard shouted. Naomi looked across the road. Ed and Richard were stood in the open doorway. They both looked exhausted. Everyone who lived in the house was to come to the door, be checked off and documented. Photographed and measured – like species in a scientific study of a dying out breed. See who was still around this time next week.

Obviously no one was mentioning Emma.

"I haven't got a Richard Stilton on my list."

"Miss Ellerbeck?"

She jumped as her own clipboard administrator pushed his face into her line of view. How dare she not pay attention. "Sorry?"

"I asked if you've come into contact with the infected?"

"No." The lie came easily and naturally; she didn't even need to think about it. Not that there was any choice. If she'd said yes, it wouldn't matter what the circumstances were. She would be transported away, a threat to the nation's health.

"Lock your door again and stay inside." He flipped over her sheet and looked to the one underneath. There was a large red cross through it. Her neighbours. Those who had been taken away the other night. Now an empty home.

Naomi backed into the corridor and closed the front door. Carefully securing all of the locks. She walked upstairs and spread her new rations out on the settee. It didn't look like very much, and was probably going to have to last several days. This would just get worse. Thank god Rudi had made her stockpile before this had turned nasty. She unscrewed one of the bottle caps, sniffed the contents and wrinkled her nose. That one would be for dire emergencies only.

Richard came to visit her an hour later, when the army patrols were safely away from their street.

"You have to let me in," he told her as she opened her door. "I have to get out of that frigging house."

She stepped back and Richard was soon past and up the stairs. She pushed the door shut. Felt growing nausea. Surely Emma wasn't still in Ed's house. They wouldn't be able to control her now. Richard wasn't infected, was he?

Naomi hurried up the stairs after him. "I got a weird phone call from Ed this morning."

"Weird is the word," Richard muttered as he flopped on to the settee.

She stepped up to the back of the settee, looking down at him. "Is she, I mean, Emma, is she infected?"

"Oh yes."

"But she's not still over there? Ed rang me up this morning saying he was going to take care of her. He wanted to know if there is a cure. We all know there isn't a cure…"

"Ed's completely switched off rationality. He thinks the cure is coming soon, and he'll keep her alive until it arrives. Christ, one way or another she'll be dead by the end of the week. She's a slavering, rabid lunatic as it is. I went down this morning to do the kind thing, but he stopped me. He thinks he's going to save her."

"But it's really dangerous," Naomi broke out. "She'll be violent, uncontrollable. You'll get bitten. You haven't already…?"

"No," Richard sighed, holding his head in his hands. "My brother has got her chained up in the back garden like a rabid dog. Fuck knows where he found those chains from. Got her tied up with a bow, all padlocked in place. He's throwing her chunks of raw steak to keep her strength up. I can not get through to him what a stupid fucking idea this is."

It sounded awful. "Would you ring the army?"

"I can't do that to my own brother. Anyway, the way things are, they'd drag all three of us off for execution. Can't take any risks."

Naomi didn't know what to say. Life in general didn't prepare you for situations like this. She walked around the settee and gingerly sat down beside him. "He must really care for her."

"That thing isn't Emma anymore. Ed's having some kind of breakdown and I don't know what to do. All I can think is that now is not the time for sentimentality."

His last comment felt like a slap in the face. She felt herself physically lean back from him. "So would you kill me if I got infected?" As soon as she had asked the question she wanted to take it back.

Richard looked at her sharply. "Would you rather turn into that thing across the road?"

Naomi looked at the floor. "No."

"Come on, it won't come to that." The deluded optimist hopes.

"What do you think you'll do?"

Richard ran a hand over his face. "I don't know. What I'm thinking is that it's time to get out of York. Get up to my place out in the middle of bloody no where. But I'm not going without Ed; Ed's not leaving Emma and I'm not taking Emma anywhere. We're at a stalemate. And in the meantime, I don't even know how we'd get out of the city. The whole place is circled by the ring road – with its half a million roundabouts with army checkpoints on every one. I don't know how we'd get across the ring road."

She felt like crying. It was selfish. Of course they wanted to get out of town. The countryside was the safest place to be, both in the immediate situation and long term. It would be cruel to begrudge anyone that hope. But when the brothers were gone, she would be completely alone with only the telephone for company; waiting until the electricity supply died and the land lines went down. She didn't know how she would cope with that kind of survival.

Richard came across as the practical type. He'd find a solution to the ring road problem. And Emma was going to die. Even with Ed's care, she only had a few days at most to go before her body collapsed under the ravages of the virus.

Naomi was staring at the wall with an expression that suggested she was about to throw up. Richard felt sorry for coming over here to dump all his problems upon her. "You need to get out of here."

She looked sadly over at him. "Out of my flat?"

"Out of York."

She shook her head. "I have no where to go."

"You can come with us if I figure out how to leave the city," Richard told her. "Seriously, this is no polite offer. I think my little village can stretch to the three of us. And you're quite handy with that bow of yours."

She managed a small smile. "I'd certainly go if you'd be prepared to take me."

"Sure. Although this is all dependent on me figuring out how to get out of here." He paused, looked at the line up of army cans on her coffee table. "You get your supplies, then?"

"Yes."

"I eventually managed to get a pack up of my own. Although it was touch and go to begin with. I wasn't on the register. They really weren't happy I was here at all."

"They didn't look that happy that they were here either."

"No, I don't suppose they would. Jesus, they must have had to clean up some crap since this all blew up." He stopped. He didn't want to think about any of it just now. "Do you mind if I crash over here a couple of hours. Ed'll ring if he needs me, which he won't. It's a bit... intense over there. I just need somewhere I can close my eyes for five minutes."

"Be my guest."

"Thank you." He smiled at her. "Oh, look, use my phone if you want to use the internet. I don't think I'm going to be the most talkative of company."

"Thanks. I'll email my friend. Let her know I'm ok."

From: naomikiwi@noworries.com.au
Sent: 05 May 12:00:19
To: teresathekoala@noworries.com.au

Subject: 05 May

Teresa,

Things are not good. Ed's girlfriend is infected and completely mental. You don't need me to tell you how people turn when they've got this – I guess you'll have seen the pictures online. Ed's not doing well either. He's not infected, but he's lost the plot. He should get the army over to deal with her, but instead he's got her tethered in the back garden and throws her raw bits of meat from the freezer to eat. He's keeping her alive.

He says they'll have a cure soon. A cure?! The last time I heard from Rudi he thought that would be years away. Besides, they say even if people are kept fed and watered, they'll only live 10-20 days before death.

Ed lives across the road from me btw. His brother, Richard, came to visit about a week ago and can't get out of York now to go home. He lives in the middle of nowhere – would be better off there.

There's nothing to do but for people to barricade themselves indoors. I'm lucky because Rudi told me to stockpile, but I don't know how other people are coping for food. We got these army supplies today – rations – but there's not much, it doesn't look appealing and they wouldn't say how long it's all supposed to last.

I don't know what else to write. It all seems a bit hopeless.

Richard wants to get out of York, but he won't go without Ed and Ed won't leave his mad girlfriend. Richard said I can go too. I don't know whether it's me or my crates of tinned pineapples he wants.

Naomi

High on Skye – the Ultimate Islander's blog

Fàilte! Or welcome. Välkommen I Skottland. Or whatever the fuck you want to say. I am the sometimes unemployed twenty something Skye resident. Raised in Portree, working when the tourists come in. Sitting on my arse through the winter. This is my life.

05 May 20--

We're screwed. Just went to the shop for some food. There's very little there. There's no supplies coming in, and no one knows how long this is going to last. Every time you go on the Internet things just look worse. It's the end of the world. We're all right – no disease, safe in our blockade. But we have no food reserves, and not that much agriculture. Skye lives on the tourist industry. What fucking tourist industry?!?!?! My old man said we'll have to live on fish and seaweed. Seaweed? For fuck's sake. And you people think you've got it bad.

Emma was looking distinctly bloated the following morning. A case of very bad trapped wind. Not that she would have been concerned that her slim figure was not at its best. She wouldn't have even understood if someone had tried to explain. Her mind had completely degenerated. She could not speak, and did not understand any form of communication. She was a wild and angry animal tethered in the back garden. Frequently she was sick or suffered from diarrhoea – more blood than any other body matter, and yet she still seemed to possess terrifying strength when she strained against her chains. She had a steady, gentle nosebleed running from her left nostril. There didn't seem to be any whites of her eyes left now; only red.

Ed was sat by the back kitchen door with a plate of hacked up pieces of raw meat. He slung them across to Emma as if he was feeding the ducks in the park. She scrabbled in the grass for the meat, greedily eating it, growling for more. The earth stank of her waste, of her drying blood seeped into the ground.

His younger brother hadn't slept in the last twenty four hours – probably the last forty eight if he was honest. He didn't even attempt a pretence of rest by going up to his bed. He sat and watched Emma and longed for a life that might have been. He didn't even seem to need to relieve himself. Richard waited and waited for him to leave the garden, if only for a few minutes, so that he could put Emma out of her misery. Ed would not move.

Richard was sat upstairs, in the front spare bedroom. Slunk forward in the wooden chair, positioned by the window, he warmed himself in the morning sun. He looked through the road atlas of the area, examining the back roads and potential routes to get home. An occasional cut through a field to avoid touching major routes – the Landrover looked rough, but it had good four wheel drive and suspension and would manage it. He'd done his share of off-roading. He had pretty much decided on his route back, if only he could think of a way to get out of York.

Lowering the map, he leant back in the chair and idly gazed out of the window. Across the road he had a direct view into Naomi's flat. She was perched in the window sill peering down at the cars parked in front of her home. Her side of the road was caught in shadows at this time of the day, and she was cast in a grainy blue-grey. Her hair was loose and she was tapping what appeared to be a hairbrush on one knee. She did seem very alone in the world. He wondered that she didn't have any family or people out there.

She stopped tapping the hairbrush on her knee and suddenly looked very melancholy. This was intrusion, and Richard felt embarrassed, as if he had purposefully gone out of his way to spy on her. He shifted his attention back to the map and pretended to himself that he had never looked.

A minute later, his gaze naturally wandered away from the road atlas again and to the world outside. He returned to her window. Naomi was staring straight back at him.

When you were watching someone in this way, it was all too easy to forget that they were living and breathing, real; not just a projected image on a screen. You could interact. And the act of spying, of voyeurism, was broken when they raised their head and met your eye.

It felt a little awkward. He got the impression she'd looked before. Ridiculous. He couldn't help himself, breaking out into a wide smile. The sharp edges of concern filtering away. Something lighter, brighter. You might have called it hope. Naomi responded in like, the smile radiating all the way up into her eyes. She brushed her hair back behind an ear.

"What the hell are you two grinning at each other like idiots for?"

Richard jumped, swerving around in the chair to find Ed stood behind him. Haggard, dishevelled, exhausted. Dark smudges under his eyes. He wore a sour expression. Sneering distaste. Richard looked back to the window, but Naomi had gone.

"Did no one mention that the world is falling apart?"

"What the hell is up with you?"

"It's all very well you sitting there making gooey eyes at her across the road." Ed waved his arms irritably at the window. "But people are dying. Emma is dying. She needs the cure." He made it sound as though there was a cure; that it was just a hold up in postal deliveries that was causing the set backs in her recovery. "Is that all you're thinking about now?"

He could hear in the tone of his voice that Ed was begging for a fight. "For Christ's sake," Richard muttered under his breath. He wasn't thinking about anything with anyone. It had just been a calm, quiet moment when he suddenly hadn't worried about anything. The rest of the world might have ceased to exist, but he wouldn't have cared, because for that second he had felt peace, happiness within. "Would you begrudge everyone a little bit of happiness? Ban hope? Without something to look forward to I don't suppose anyone could find the energy to struggle through this trying to survive."

"And what are you looking forward to? White picket fences?"

Richard looked bitterly at his brother. "You need to sleep."

"Not while you're here."

"Well, I'm planning on leaving soon."

"Leaving?" A touch of aggression left Ed's voice, replaced by nerves. "What do you mean leaving?"

"I'm going back home. I haven't completely figured out how yet, but I'm leaving York. You're coming with me."

"But what about Emma? I can't leave her."

"Emma's going nowhere."

"I can't leave her. Besides, you don't know how you're going to get out of York, do you? They'll have got a cure to us by the time you've figured that out. Then all three of us can get out to your place. You know what; I think she might actually have improved a bit since last night."

Richard looked miserably across to Naomi's empty window as Ed hurried back down the stairs to check on

Emma. Ed was completely deluded. And yet perhaps there was a prediction in all of that. They'll have got a cure to us by the time he'd figured out how to get out of York. Maybe neither was ever going to happen.

From: teresathekoala@noworriesnet.com.au
Sent: 06 May 20-- 14:45:46
To: naomikiwi@noworriesnet.com.au

Subject: RE: 05 May

Naomi,

What do you mean you don't know whether it's you or the pineapple chunks? This hardly sounds like the time to be chasing men. Although if he can get you out to a safe house, he may be worth latching on to.

You do surprise me. You've been single for years. What a time to break a habit. So, what's the gossip?

I am officially with Shane now btw. He's great. I love the Australian sense of humour. We went to a barbi yesterday. Weather's not too bad. Sorry, I shouldn't be writing about stuff like that to you.

Teresa

From: naomikiwi@noworriesnet.com.au
Sent: 06 May 18:10:00
To: teresathekoala@noworriesnet.com.au

Subject: 06 May pm

I am not latching on to him. He is not after my pineapples and I am not after him for his safe house.

Gossip? This isn't a fucking soap opera.

He passed her a boiled sweet and told her it was for afterwards.

Naomi looked at the object in her hands. It was a mint humbug; caramel coloured with dark brown stripes, wrapped up in a twist of clear plastic. Sweets like this would only last as long as supplies that were already produced. Opening up the confectionary factories again was not going to be on the top of anyone's priorities.

She picked up the empty jerry can and removed the cap. Richard had unscrewed the fuel cap on the side of her car. He was feeding the length of hosepipe into the petrol cap. Naomi set the container by his side. Richard put the other end of the hosepipe into his mouth. There was a moment or two of silence, then he grimaced, pulling the pipe from his mouth and into the container.

He spat a mouthful of petrol and saliva onto the ground. "Jesus."

"Not recommended?" Naomi passed him the humbug.

"No." He put the sweet in his mouth, pushing the wrapper in his trouser pocket.

"And Emma?"

He looked across at Naomi from under his eyebrows. "Still alive."

Still alive. Naomi looked over at Ed's house. It was now four days since Emma had been bitten. It was amazing that her body had not collapsed from exhaustion. Strange that no one had reported her. Certainly Ed would not because he was convinced she would be saved; Richard would not because it would effectively sign his and Ed's death sentences as well, but surely the neighbours would have noticed.

The house to the left of Ed's was now empty. The man who had lived there had been killed on that sunny day that felt like decades ago. The neighbours on the other side, she didn't know. She had seen occasional movement earlier, but in the last couple of days the house had become a shell. As if the residents had ceased to exist. Their part of the street had become intensely silent. It was as if she, Richard, Ed and Emma were the only people left alive: all in varying states of decay.

There was a sharp high scream from further down the residential street. Both Naomi and Richard instinctively ducked for cover down the side of her car.

"What was that?" Naomi whispered.

Richard was pulling the hosepipe out of the car. "I don't know," he said quietly, working swiftly. "But I think now is the time to get in doors."

The pipe was removed from the car, the fuel cap screwed back in place. With petrol container in hand, he followed Naomi over the short distance to her front door. They hurried inside, slamming the door shut and turning all the locks. Richard put the jerry can down on the mat and screwed on the lid.

"No, you won't take me!" a woman screamed.

Naomi and Richard exchanged a look. This had been happening more and more frequently. Their street was quiet, through traffic only occasional. They read about much more online. Suddenly anyone who was able was desperately documenting everything on blogs, forums and websites. Eyewitness accounts, photographs, videos, even disjointed sound files recording the screams and guttural primeval noises of the badly infected.

Naomi leaned up to the door and peered out of the spy hole. A woman stumbled into view. Her clothes were torn and heavily bloodstained. She was red in the face from exertion. Clearly terrified. Everyone knew that anyone suspected of carrying the disease was routinely executed. There wasn't any treatment available, and they were too much of an infection risk to be allowed to continue. No one, not even the army were trying to pretend now.

A soldier came into view, followed by a second. Full battle gear, going in to war to fight the enemy. They both had powerful looking guns – Naomi knew nothing about modern weaponry and couldn't identify them – strapped to their bodies, held in shoot position. Two fully armed, fully armoured men against one defenceless, terrified woman.

"Leave me alone!"

"Take her down!"

There was a neat bang, and her head exploded in a crimson waterfall. The spray glittered in the sunlight. She dropped like a rag doll failing on starter's orders. Naomi gasped and turned away from the door in a panic, bumping into Richard. He pulled her to him, cradling her in his arms. She was quite content to close her eyes and bury her face in his shirt, hoping somehow it might erase all those images.

People were terrified, and no one wanted to admit to the army that they might be infected. Runners were on the increase, hoping they could escape capture. It only fuelled the spread of infection. Street executions of this style were frequently witnessed. Bodies piled up. The usual crematoriums couldn't cope with the influx, and deep pits had to be dug. The diseased dead were tossed in and a match was lit. Last night the light from the fields around the Monks Cross shopping area had given the night sky a sickly orange tinge.

"When will we go?" Naomi mumbled.

"In the night," he replied. "As soon as Emma's dead. I can't get Ed away from her while she's still alive." He paused. "She looked pregnant this morning."

"What?" She looked horrified.

He shook his head. "Swollen abdomen. You know what's going on in there."

She didn't want to think about it.

"Wee small hours we'll set off," Richard reiterated. It had all been decided. When it was dark, when the ungodly hours after midnight were upon them, they would leave. The Landrover was virtually packed; most of Naomi's food stocks piled in the back of the vehicle, the tarpaulin thrown over the top. Innocently waiting.

Richard had spent the last two days watching the patrol's routine in the area. The route they took. The frequency of visits had dropped – there were more runaways and riots to deal with, what with there only having been one more meagre food delivery yesterday.

The escape route had been planned on the maps, Naomi drawing in the essential tracks they would need to get out of York and head north into the countryside. Extra rations of petrol had now been drained from her and Ed's cars, ready to be taken with their other supplies when they left. She had a rucksack of essential items packed – all the space she could afford for herself. Everything else would stay in the flat, locked up. Maybe one day she would return here, maybe not. It was hard to imagine what any kind of future they might have.

She had called her mother and Rudi to tell them she hoped to be leaving town in the next few days with friends. Any worry of going against rules and army decrees were far outweighed by the relieving prospect of being safer; being away from centres of population. Rudi of course was in the worst possible place to be – central London – but security was so thorough, he said the only place he was going to get the disease from was the specimens they purposefully brought in. And still Scotland remained disease free. A few had tried to cross the now heavily guarded borders, but were shot: either killed outright, maimed, or scared back into the nightmare. Her mother, living in southern Scotland, was relatively safe for the time being.

Richard waited until the soldiers had left before returning to Ed's house. The body lay in the street – the clean-up crews unable to keep up with the killings these days. It would be hours before they'd arrive to deal with the biohazard.

Naomi went upstairs and settled on the settee. Time to wait.

From: teresathekoala@noworriesnet.com.au
Sent: 08 May 20-- 14:22:13
To: naomikiwi@noworriesnet.com.au

Subject: My brother

I don't think this is a soap opera.

I spoke to my mum a couple of days. It was just after I got your email. My brother is dead. He took an overdose. Apparently it's becoming quite a popular thing to do. My mum and dad are talking about it. Even if they don't get infected, they don't think there'll be a Britain worth living in after all of this is finished.

I don't know what to say or think anymore. I don't know if you'll even read this. Maybe you've topped yourself as well. Teresa

Emma was dead.

Sometime in the morning she had died. It had not been an easy death. Even now, she was on her back, still chained up in the garden. Her abdomen had burst, and all the rotting blood and liquefied organs had splattered around her in one final desperate attempt to spread the infection. She had died alone, unaware of her solitude or her state, for her mind was completely lost, a skull full of overcooked vegetables. There she lay, and even the flies didn't seem to want to come and pick over the remains.

Richard had returned to find Ed crumpled on the kitchen floor, sobbing for Emma. He tried to console his brother, but Ed, who couldn't recall the last time he had slept, had punched Richard in the face and told him to get out. Richard had backed off. He told Ed they were leaving that night, at one, and to try and get some rest before then. He would be across the road with Naomi if he needed anything.

Ed keeled over in front of the washing machine and lay there in a blubbering stupor for many hours. He eventually drifted off into a restless, horrible sleep filled with bloody images and nightmares. It was all over.

It was growing dark when he woke up. The kitchen was silent apart from the hum of the fridge. Ed sat up and listened to nothing. He checked the kitchen clock – it was only eight in the evening. Richard was probably still over with Naomi. Did they do this on purpose to torment him? Suddenly now they needed their secret little group of two, just when Emma had left him.

Opening the kitchen door, he went out into the back garden. It was quite a chilly night. Her corpse was festering in place, the look on agony caught in what remained of her expression. Bloodied remains. It really wasn't fair. She'd had so much to live for. He'd been pinning all these hopes and ambitions on her, half of which he wouldn't have even admitted to himself. And he'd come up with the stupid idea that she would be safer here, that she should hurry through this pestilence-infested town to come to his home. If he hadn't have suggested that, she would be alive now. Everything would be different.

"Oh, Emma," he cried, stumbling up to her body and dropping to his knees. It had just been the beginning. They'd never known intimacy. He'd never even been able to kiss her. He'd tried to keep her fit. Fed her at all hours of the day. Just waiting for that cure that did not arrive. His head was spinning.

He needed to be closer. He scrambled on all fours so that he was over her, astride her. Emma's dead eyes stared off to the far corner of the garden. No comment. She wouldn't hurt a fly. He shouldn't have chained her up in the back garden like a rabid dog. What an undignified way to go. And now she was dead and there was no point in living. There was nothing to look forward to. The world was over.

A tear dropped onto her face. He put his hands in the pools of blood and excrement. Ran a finger down the side of her heavily blotched face. Kissed her forehead. Gave up to abandon and dropped himself into her, wrapping his limbs around her decaying form; burying his face into her blood-stiffen curls. Breathed in the stench. Tasted the blood. Stayed there for hours.

It was pitch black when he rose from the dead. There were no thoughts left in his mind. He got up and walked back into the house, shutting the door behind him. Saw the time on the clock. It was almost midnight. Leaving his shoes by the back kitchen door, he walked upstairs and into the bathroom. Turned on the shower and felt the steam fill the room. He took off the blood-stained clothes one by one and put them into the washing basket – as if they ever would be made clean again. Stepped into the shower as he faintly heard the front door go. Richard's voice but he couldn't make out the words.

Ed got into the shower and closed his eyes as the water pounded onto his body. The filth ran down in rivers, twisting into the plughole and away. He stayed there for a long time, feeling the water wash him clean, remove all but the smallest of traces of Emma.

When he was satisfied, he turned off the shower. Dripping, he walked through to his bedroom and selected clean, crisp clothes from the wardrobe. He dressed like he was going to an interview; everything but the tie. Work shoes. Looked in the mirror and saw a dead man. It was time to go.

Naomi was already in the passenger seat when Ed came out of the house. Richard's Landrover was packed with as much food and supplies as they could fit in; Naomi's bows, cans of petrol and a few personal possessions. She'd taken one last walk around her flat that evening, making sure all the windows were locked, electrical items unplugged. As if this was just a short holiday and she would be back soon. She had locked the front door and pocketed the keys.

She felt the vehicle dip slightly as Ed climbed up onto the back and dropped down on top of the tarpaulin. Richard walked to the back of the vehicle and shared a muttered conversation with his brother before returning to the cab. He climbed into the driver's seat and shut the door. Naomi felt that she was intruding on a private family affair. "Is he all right?" she asked quietly. It seemed like a stupid question. Emma had recently died, and now they were fleeing York like refugees – but refugees knowing there wasn't really anywhere safe left in the world. Certainly no where they could get to.

Richard stared steadily out of the windscreen. "I don't know."

He started the engine, mentally reminding himself not to turn on the headlights, and quietly rolled out of the drive.

They weren't completely sure that the planned escape route was going to work, but having studied the local maps and gone through the alternatives, Naomi's suggestion had stood forth as the clear winner. After all, since the outbreak, she had managed to cross the ring road on foot without being caught – by the authorities at least – and was sure the route was passable for a vehicle that could be driven off road.

Turning left, they drove slowly up the main road towards a skewed cross junction. In some ways this was the most nerve wracking, for it was the main roads in the area that the army patrols were regularly using. Richard had been watching the patrols and worked out as best he could when he thought it would be safe to travel. Beyond that they simply had to hold their breath and hope for the best.

Travelling over the crossroad, he turned onto the road through the old village. A few metres up and they heard screaming – somewhere in the area, but impossible to say where it was now or where it was going. Richard pulled the Landrover up onto the edge of someone's drive and turned off the engine.

"Get down," he told Naomi; hoping his brother would have enough sense to remain in the horizontal position of abject misery he had been determined to travel in.

Naomi ducked down, disappearing from view of the windows. Richard hunkered down, peering over the edge of the back window. Behind them, where the main road crossed by perpendicular, two figures ran past, arms flailing. They were soon followed by a small group of people. There were shouts and growls. Obviously one side was infected, the other disease free, but Richard wouldn't have liked to have guessed which was which.

"What was that all about?" Naomi had sat up a little to watch out of the window.

"I don't want to know." Richard turned the engine on and pulled out of the driveway. He continued up through the old village road, past darkened, soundless houses and homes with character, now devoid of soul. If anyone still lived on this road, they didn't want to be seen, and wouldn't come to the window to see who was driving past. They'd probably just presume it was the army. The attempts of getting out of town had fizzled out since the original panicked rush and riots. It was presumed that if someone was going to run, they would have tried it by now.

Naomi nudged him as they reached the single track lane to the left leading down to the river. At the end, crossing over a little bridge, he pulled into an empty dirt car park in front of a country church complete with spire, yew trees and walled churchyard. There was a gate at the far side of the car park leading into a field.

"We need to go through there," Naomi said, her hand on the door. "I'll go open the gate."

He wasn't happy letting her get out in the dark to open the gates, but the driver had to stay in the vehicle to be able to move quickly. Richard reached behind her seat and pulled out a pair of bolt cutters.

"Jesus, where did you get these from?"

"If there's a padlock or any chains, just cut through with these. You're not to hang around."

"Ok."

As it turned out, there was a rudimentary fastening device of tied thick string. Naomi opened the gate and pushed it wide. As Richard drove through she pushed the gate to behind him. It was strange being out at this time in the morning. It was darker than usual, some of the street lamps not appearing to work anymore. So intensely quiet except for the occasional screams and shouts. Distant bursts of gun shot. The last time she had walked through here the sun had been blazing.

She scrambled back into the passenger seat and shut the door. Her heart was throwing itself against her ribs.

"Ok, you're going to have to guide me a bit here. I don't want to put the lights on." The moon was out, and it was possible to see a little, but now that they had pulled away from built up areas and the street lighting that was still working, they were throwing themselves upon the mercy of darkness. Anything could be out there.

"You want to head diagonally left away from the river. In the corner of the field there's a gap in the back hedge. You can drive through there, then straight up the side of that field till you get to a farm track."

The Landrover leaned and lunged as he drove over the uneven field. A hedge leered up in front of them with no way through.

"We must be too far down."

"We'll follow this down to the back of the field." He put the vehicle in reverse and for a moment it refused to move, needing to back up and over a ridge of earth. He swore under his breath and put his foot on the accelerator. He had been aiming for a gentle ride with as few revs as possible. This was early in the morning, and the usual noise of life – transport and people going about their business – had essentially been cut out. Everything was painfully loud and obvious.

The Landrover rolled quickly backwards, leaping back out of the dip. Richard swung it around and drove up beside the hedge until they reached the back corner. Across to the left he could make out the gap Naomi had mentioned. Driving through, he continued in a relatively straight line until the ground levelled out and the sound of clear earth and grit against tyres were clear.

"Need to go right."

The Landrover swung around to the right and followed the farm track through the blackness. Naomi leaned forward, squinting through the night and trying to work out just how far they had come. When she was sure she had seen the farm sheds, she waved her hand at Richard to signal him to slow down.

"The track goes past these buildings, then rolls down to the ring road. There's a bit of a slope immediately opposite to get into the fields on the other side."

"Farm track on both sides?"

She nodded.

He switched off the engine. "And this crossing place is within sight of one of the roundabouts."

She nodded. "But there's no lamps by the road. They won't see us."

"I don't want to give them any reason to look this way. We're going to push our way over." He looked over at her. "You drive."

"Me? But I...?"

"You're the lightest. Anyway, it won't be difficult." He opened the driver's door and got out. "Scoot across. Look, it's easy. We won't be going fast. Keep in neutral and steer it. When we get to the peak of this slope put the brake on. I want to go and check the road's clear. Then we'll use the speed on the roll down to get us up the other side."

"I'm not a great driver."

"You'll be fine. I'll take over later on if you want. But for now, you're in control. I'll go get my brother out the back."

Pushing the door shut, leaving Naomi on her own in the cab in the dark, Richard walked down the length of the silent vehicle and tugged at his brother's leg. "Get out," he told him. "We need to push this over the road."

Ed slowly sat up. "You've run out of petrol?"

"No. We're crossing enemy lines."

Ed slid to the back of the Landrover and hopped down to the ground. "Let's get this over with."

They pushed the Landrover forward, rolling easily onwards. Naomi rolled down the window and put her arm out to let them know they were stopping at the top of the slope. Richard went on ahead, surprised by just how nervous he was. Over the last few days he had been out of the house skulking in the local area, watching the army's movements, and quite surprised that no one had noticed him. Perhaps they weren't expected anyone to try and flee this way.

Reaching the edge of the road, he listened for the sound of running vehicles using the ring road and heard nothing. To his right it was darkness; to his left he could see the lights surrounding the roundabout. The blockades and trucks; occasional movement of a figure.

They quickly pushed the Landrover across the road and up the slope into the fields on the other side. Relief when they passed the trees that lined the edge of the road, swinging towards the right to go through a gap in the hedge into another field. When the vehicle was up on level ground again, Ed pulled himself up into the back of the Landrover and refused to be of any more help.

Richard climbed into the passenger seat. Naomi looked over at him, clearly worried. "Do I just start the engine now? Won't they hear?"

"We'll be fine. Let's just get going."

"I've never driven anything this big." She reached for the keys in the ignition and turned them, cringing as the sound of the motor starting seemed to boom out through the night like a bomb exploding. Easing her foot off the clutch, they started forward again.

Following the rough track up the edge of the field, she drove forward through the full length, slipping across a wide space where hedging should have been, going into a field to their left. Up in the top corner of this there was another wide gate blocking the way into a rough, single lane green track.

Richard got out with the bolt cutters and strode to the gate. Naomi watched as he checked the fastenings, giving the gate a shake before giving up and taking the bolt cutters to the lock. Pushing the gate back around into the hedge, he came back to the Landrover.

"I can't wait to put the gate back behind us," he told her as he got into the passenger seat. "Stuff the country code. I just want to get going."

"I know what you mean." She clamped her shaking hand around the gear stick and stared straight ahead. She could do this. The worst was over, she reminded herself; they had actually crossed over the ring road, and were heading out into the countryside.

The green track up between hedged fields gradually grew in condition as they neared the sewerage works. Just before there, she noted the gap in the hedge to her right, where she had walked down to the river. Somewhere in that field, the man had attacked her and she had knocked him to the ground. Perhaps his body was still there, rotting in the grass.

The track evened out and headed towards the edge of Haxby – a large residential area to the north of York. Houses began to loom out of the darkness, the track filtering into a tarmac road. Ahead there was a T-junction where they joined the main road out of Haxby. As she pulled out to go right, old habits would not die and she looked left to check for coming traffic. In the middle of the road there was a gathering, hunched down like animals, crowding and snuffling.

"What...?"

They couldn't help but gaze out with curiosity. There was an object lying in the road, with three of figures scrabbling around, pulling at things and putting them into their mouths.

One of the figures looked up at the Landrover, a woman with a scratched face, her skin a sickly shade under the street light. Her mouth looked like a giant gaping hole due to the flush of thick drying blood that was slopped down her chin. She put her hands into the carcass and pulled out some raw meat.

"Drive," Richard whispered.

Naomi felt her throat tighten. "Is that a...?"

"Drive. Now." He pushed at her shoulder, as if pushing her would make the Landrover move faster.

Naomi swung the vehicle round and drove away from the scene, picking up speed as the houses flashed by. The sudden influx of light, that which there was, seemed to burn at her eyes, imbedding images in her brain. "That was a person on the ground. They were eating a body." She wanted to throw up. She knew this was happening. She'd read so much on the Internet, studied the horror stories. She'd even seen attacks and executions outside her own home. Yet there was something sickening about the quiet feeding conducted in that road; the pack scavenger atmosphere. The way those hands had curled into a human carcass and ripped out the still-warm meat.

Her eyes started to well up as she drove away from the last houses and into the countryside and the darkness again.

"I can't."

Richard looked behind them as the Landrover slowed. No one was following. In fact, those figures hadn't even attempted to get up when they'd driven by. Strange considering the infection made people psychotic. Perhaps they were satisfied with the feed they had.

"We'll swap," he told her, getting out of the now stationary vehicle. He jogged around the front as Naomi shifted her body through the cab. Clambering into the driver's seat, he put his foot down and sped away further from Haxby. He didn't want to linger anywhere.

As agreed from studying the map, he drove straight onwards, ignoring the sharp turn to the right that the only through-road took. Heading straight upwards, they came to a farm and a dead end. Richard drove through a short section of field before reaching the railway. Forcing the Landrover up the gravel and up to the tracks, he drove with one side of wheels inside, one out of the tracks, up the railway, heading towards the next settlement further north of York – Strensall. Here they couldn't have afforded to switch to the local roads as Strensall had army barracks. If they were caught by the army patrols now, considering what little patience the army and police had left, they would not be taken back to their homes and warned not to do it again. Richard didn't want to think what was being done to obstructive rebels.

Following the railway through the village, he continued until the tracks crossed over a country road at the top of an area of open heath land common. At this level crossing he pulled back onto the road. God only knew what this journey was doing to his suspension and tyres, but as long as he got home, he didn't care.

From this point, the plan was to follow the country back roads up north until they reached a suitable point, already settled upon, to cross over the A road – a stretch of dual carriageway hopefully unused as they crossed straight over – to continue along the little back roads on a winding and convoluted way to Richard's house in a small, isolated village where, he prayed to God, there had been no outbreak of the HEMO10 virus.

Naomi wiped at her eyes with the sleeve of her shirt. Twisting in her seat, she looked out of the back of the Landrover. She could make out Ed's slumped figure stretched out on top of the tarpaulin. Not a comfortable position, she imagined, but Ed seemed to be stretched out as if perfectly relaxed. As if he didn't care anymore. Beyond him was the road, faded and disappearing into darkness. And for a moment she thought she saw a figure, something, running after them, but that couldn't be, because Richard was driving quite fast and there was no one out here. They had driven beyond the virus, she told herself, and hoped that she would never have to come into contact with it again.

In the back of the vehicle, Ed sighed and rolled onto his side.